SPECIAL MESSAGE TO READERS

This book is published under the auspices of

THE ULVERSCROFT FOUNDATION

(registered charity No. 264873 UK)

Established in 1972 to provide funds for research, diagnosis and treatment of eye diseases. Examples of contributions made are: —

A Children's Assessment Unit at Moorfield's Hospital, London.

•

Twin operating theatres at the Western Ophthalmic Hospital, London.

•

A Chair of Ophthalmology at the Royal Australian College of Ophthalmologists.

•

The Ulverscroft Children's Eye Unit at the Great Ormond Street Hospital For Sick Children, London.

You can help further the work of the Foundation by making a donation or leaving a legacy. Every contribution, no matter how small, is received with gratitude. Please write for details to:

THE ULVERSCROFT FOUNDATION,
The Green, Bradgate Road, Anstey,
Leicester LE7 7FU, England.
Telephone: (0116) 236 4325

In Australia write to:
THE ULVERSCROFT FOUNDATION,
c/o The Royal Australian and New Zealand
College of Ophthalmologists,
94-98 Chalmers Street, Surry Hills,
N.S.W. 2010, Australia

SHOWDOWN AT DANE'S BEND

Sam Limbo, innocent but jailed for murder, is forced to remain in Dane's Bend, a powder-keg town. The townsfolk are awaiting the arrival of the notorious Donovan brothers, intent on avenging the killing of the youngest Donovan. The brothers have a big interest in the bank which, with a secret stash, has taken on hired private security. Limbo breaks out of jail, but returns, lured by the marshal's daughter. And it's Limbo who saves the town that wanted to hang him.

Books by Jack Holt
in the Linford Western Library:

GUNHAWK'S REVENGE
PETTICOAT MARSHAL
HOT LEAD RANGE
HARD RIDE TO LARGO
DANGLING NOOSE

JACK HOLT

SHOWDOWN AT DANE'S BEND

Complete and Unabridged

LINFORD
Leicester

First published in Great Britain in 2008 by
Robert Hale Limited
London

First Linford Edition
published 2009
by arrangement with
Robert Hale Limited
London

British Library CIP Data

Holt, Jack.
Showdown at Dane's Bend- -
(Linford western library)
1. Western stories.
2. Large type books.
I. Title II. Series
823.9′2–dc22

ISBN 978–1–84782–811–8

Published by
F. A. Thorpe (Publishing)
Anstey, Leicestershire

Set by Words & Graphics Ltd.
Anstey, Leicestershire
Printed and bound in Great Britain by
T. J. International Ltd., Padstow, Cornwall

This book is printed on acid-free paper

1

'I figure that last ace, like the one before, came from up your sleeve, friend.' Sam Limbo's voice was barely audible, and yet it had the volume of priarie thunder. The accused man's reaction was one of scoffing dismissiveness which, in Limbo's experience, had often been the retort of a man bent on bluffing away the trouble he was in. He reached for the pot. Sam Limbo gripped his wrists. 'Ain't yours to take, mister,' he said. 'In fact none of the last four pots were yours to take. So I figure that you should put your winnings back on the table to be shared out among the men you've cheated.'

'I haven't cheated anyone,' the man said, in a tone that suggested he had had more schooling than most men of the West. His silk waistcoat and tailored garb suggested a professional man. Of course, he might just be a no-good tinhorn dressed up to look like something he was not, when in fact he was a professional gambler by trade. Many of that ilk were smooth talkers and flash dressers. 'I don't agree. And what's more I don't intend to comply. That pot's mine by right, and I'll thank you to hand it over, sir.'

Sam Limbo shook his head.

'As you'd say, I don't intend to comply, friend.'

The expensively dressed man's eyes became vulture mean. The seconds dragged while he considered the situation. Tension spread around the table with the swiftness of a rattler's spit, and chairs began to slide back from the table, leaving a clear path between the man who had made the charge and the accused gambler.

'Now,' said the tall stranger with the steely blue eyes, 'I can take it from your pockets when you're dead. The choice is yours, mister.'

Time in the saloon seemed to stand

still on the second it was in, and the honky-tonk piano finished on a note that was at odds with those gone before. The men who had been in the game of blackjack sprang from their chairs and joined the patrons crowding the bar, well out of the way of the gunfire which now seemed inevitable.

'Don't aim to wait too long,' the stranger to Dane's Bend warned the cheat.

Everyone in Dane's Bend had suspected for a long time that Benjamin Archer, the town legal eagle, cheated at cards, but on two accounts had been reluctant to say so. Firstly because he was a very good and very slick cheat. And secondly, no one, including Marshal Andy Daly, would have given any credence to a charge of cheating because Archer moved in the right social circles, unlike those who sat at the gambling tables with him.

'Archer, a card-sharp,' Daly had said, only the day before when Archer's consistent and incredible run of good fortune had gone on longer than any lucky streak could have. 'Why would Archer want to cheat at cards? He must have the fattest bank balance in town.'

'Sometimes it ain't the money that counts,' the complainant had said. 'It's just that some cheats can't help themselves. It's a kinda head sickness, Andy.'

Marshal Andy Daly had dismissed the man's charge out of hand. 'Benjamin Archer's no cheat. Take my word for it. You're just upset 'cause you've got only the lining left in your pockets.'

The man reckoned that he'd save his breath, because he hadn't the price of a beer to slake his thirst. Besides, he reckoned that he could keep on gabbing until his voice wore out and he would not convince the marshal of Benjamin Archer's crookedness at a card table.

Gathering his wits, Archer decided to rebuff the stranger's claim. 'I'm of a mind to send for Marshal Daly to seek justice and retribution, sir,' he declared indignantly. 'However, if you'll just drop your impetuous accusation and apologize, I'm of a mind to be charitable.'

'Never did hear so many ten-dollar words strung together before,' Limbo intoned. 'But in my book you're still a lowdown skunk of a cheat! And I aim to prove it.'

Shaken, but still considering that he held the upper hand on the drifter, Archer said, 'And how might you do as you say?'

'By . . . ' In a lightning fast gesture, the stranger grabbed Archer's arm and ripped the sleeve of his coat to reveal a spring mechanism that still held two aces, activated by Archer's wrist pressing on the table to slide an ace into his hand, 'showing the good folk here how you cheat.'

Knowing the game was up, Archer sprang up and upended the table. A derringer flashed in his hand, but a second too late. He was fast, much faster than Limbo had anticipated he would be and he had almost been out-foxed. But, as Archer tumbled backwards, his eyes fixed on the hole in his chest, all hell broke loose in the saloon, and by the time the place was quietened down by the appearance of Marshal Andy Daly a couple of minutes later, the derringer had been secreted away and the charge against Archer's accuser was one of murdering an unarmed man. Furthermore, there was no shortage of witnesses who stepped forward to state so.

'What's your name, stranger?' Daly's demand was backed up by a primed shotgun.

'Limbo, Marshal. Sam Limbo.'

'Well, it looks like you're gallows bound, Limbo,' Daly said.

'It was a fair fight, Marshal. That fella was a cheat. I challenged him. He drew a derringer on me, and I defended myself.' Sam Limbo held the lawman's gaze. 'Like I said. A fair fight.'

'Archer being a cheat, I'll give you,' Daly was forced to concede, because there was no denying it now that he had seen the mechanism strapped to the former lawyer's right arm. 'But in my book, being a card cheat ain't reason enough to kill a man in cold blood, Limbo. And that's what you just did.'

The marshal stymied Sam Limbo's protestations.

'Ain't no sign of this derringer you talk about.'

Sam Limbo's eyes swept the saloon, but every eye he met looked away. 'It's as plain as the nose on your face, Marshal, that during the confusion, someone hid the derringer away.'

Andy Daly was unconvinced. 'Who'd want to go to all that bother?'

'Beats me,' Sam Limbo confessed. 'But that's surely what happened.'

'Anyone see this derringer?' Daly called out. No answer came back.

'Are you all blind?' Limbo charged the crowd.

A man to the front of the crowd spoke up.

'Benjamin Archer was a citizen of this town, mister,' he stated. 'And you're a no-good saddle-bum.' There was the kernel of his problem, Limbo reckoned.

'Benjamin was also a cheat who's been robbing you blind,' Limbo responded. 'Ain't any man in this dungheap of a town got pride?'

'Two things you need, Limbo,' the marshal said. 'Evidence, like that derringer, and witnesses to say that it was, as you say, a fair fight. You ain't got neither. So all I can say is that you tell your story to the judge. If he believes you, you won't swing. But if he don't, you sure as hell will, friend.'

He prodded Limbo with the shotgun.

'Now, move!'

For a moment, Sam Limbo gave consideration to challenging the marshal's style of law-keeping but, sensibly, only for a moment. He had been in enough towns (most of which he had been run out of simply because drifting ways to most folk equated with criminal leanings) to know that the law in any particular town was what the lawman in that town reckoned it should be. And he had also learned, from tough experience and hard knocks, that a drifter's word was worthless.

'I reckon you should just march the saddle trash along to that fine oak at the end of Main and sling a rope, Marshal,' said one of the gamblers who had moments before sat at the table with Limbo, and for whom he had demanded that Archer should make restitution.

It was a mid-week night, lacking in excitement, and a hanging would surely fill a low point in the week. That became evident from the enthusiastic support for the man's opinion.

'We'll have enough of that,' Andy Daly rebuked the suggester's enthusiastic supporters. 'The only one who can order a hanging is a judge.'

The lawman's feisty stance had Sam Limbo thinking that the miracle he had missed out on in a hundred previous towns might have happened in the rotting town of Dane's Bend — lo and behold, an honest lawman?

'Start walking,' Daly ordered Sam Limbo.

The marshal's stance left no doubt that if he had to, he would not hesitate to pull the triggers of the blaster. Being a man who liked breathing more than most things, Sam Limbo headed for the batwings. Nearing the exit from the saloon, a knife thudded into the frame of one of the batwings. Sam Limbo swung around, his eyes scanning the crowd from which impassive faces looked back.

'Leave it be, mister,' Daly warned.

'Ain't you going to find out who threw that knife, Marshal?' Limbo challenged the marshal. 'Or is there one law for strangers and another law for citizens in this burg?' he added, with even greater challenge.

'You seem to be the kind of fella who's always on the prod for trouble,' Daly said between clenched teeth. 'Well, if it's trouble you want, it's trouble you'll get.'

Sam Limbo's brain reverberated from the blow of the shotgun butt. He fought gallantly to stay upright. But from the second butt met bone, it was a fight he was bound to lose. He came to groggily when two burly men threw him into a cell in the jail, like they might a dead carcass of no great value.

Through a haze that had all the colours of the rainbow, Sam Limbo saw the marshal slam the cell door shut.

Its clang had the ring of a death knell to it.

'I've got a bottle in my desk drawer, gents,' Daly said. 'I reckon we could kill it off 'tween us.' Limbo could do with a drink, but asking, he reckoned, would not give it to him. Sam Limbo curled up on the bunk and let the darkness engulf him, not sure at that point if he would ever again return from it.

2

A bright, eye-numbing spot of light that grew ever bigger and ever more intense was Sam Limbo's introduction to the following morning. The light turned orange and was something of a mystery, before Limbo recognized it as the sun cresting the hills above the town, ushering in another day, a day he would much prefer to forego. The rattle of a tin cup and plate reminded Limbo of how hungry he was. That he could recall, in a head that was still spinning from the contact with the walnut butt of the marshal's shotgun the previous night; he had not had solid food inside him in three days. The tin plate of piping hot ham and eggs the woman at the other side of the bars was holding, added to her red-haired, green-eyed beauty, almost made consciousness pleasant. He pinched himself to make sure that he was awake and not dreaming.

'Just a minute,' the apparition said, when Limbo reached for the plate of food.

The woman placed the tin plate on the floor and went to the marshal's desk to pick up the shotgun that had sent him into oblivion. She came back pointing the blaster.

'Just in case you get any notions,' she said. 'So, if you want your breakfast, you'll step back to the wall before I open the cell door, and remain there until I close it again.'

'I'd appreciate it, ma'am, if you'd point that blaster downwards,' Limbo said. 'It might just go off.'

'If it does, I reckon you'll be no loss to anyone.'

Sam Limbo held up his hands. 'I'm backing off, lady.'

'Right against the wall,' the woman said, when Limbo left a small gap between him and the wall.

'You sure are a bossy kind of woman,' he said.

'Do as you're told, and I can be real sweet-natured.'

'You know, ma'am, I'd like to see that sweet nature you talk of. But I reckon I ain't going to live to be a hundred.'

'Move a muscle when I open this door,' she said, grittily, 'and you won't live a second longer. That's a promise.'

'You married?'

'No. Why?'

'Well, if you were, I was about to dig into my chest of dusty prayers to ask the Lord to be kind and take your man quickly.'

The woman stared him down. 'You want breakfast?'

'Yes, ma'am.'

'Then I would suggest that you use your mouth for eating and eating alone.'

'Whatever you say, ma'am.'

'And don't call me ma'am. I ain't that old.'

'Hardly out of swaddling clothes, I'd say.'

'I'm not interested in what you have

to say. And I'm not interested in your smarmy talk either.' She opened the cell door and, keeping a keen eye on Limbo, placed the breakfast plate and tin cup inside the cell. 'Stay put!' the woman ordered when, hunger overtaking all else, Sam Limbo went to claim the piping hot and extremely aromatic food.

He held up his hands.

'It's just that my insides are hollow, ma'am. Miss,' he corrected quickly under the woman's frosty glare.

'You can have it when I lock the cell door,' she said, pointing the shotgun in a fashion that Sam Limbo reckoned was evidence of her ability to use the gun. 'Not a second before,' she added, scowling.

Limbo thought that, even scowling like a displeased schoolmarm, she was still the prettiest skirt he had set eyes on since a woman he had dallied with for a spell the previous year, until one day, poking around in the barn he had found the ragged remains of her husband — well, at least he reckoned that it was her husband, but it could also have been another man of whom she had tired. He did not go back to the house and wake her up to enquire. He had saddled up and hit the trail, curbing his latest bout of desire for her, because in his experience in his wide travels, a woman with a killer's instinct was infinitely more dangerous than a man with the same leanings. That brought him to speculating about the woman standing before him now. If he tried to get past her, would she really pull the triggers of the shotgun?

Looking deep into her green eyes, flinty as stone, Sam Limbo concluded that it was a chance he'd prefer not to take — at least not on an empty stomach. There would be other opportunities to escape — there always were.

She slammed the cell door shut and turned the key in the lock.

'Thanks, miss,' Limbo said, diving for the food.

'When did you last eat?' she asked, in

a not unkindly way.

'Three days ago,' Limbo answered, between devouring what was on the plate. 'This burg serves up good grub.' He chuckled. 'Might decide to hang around for a while.'

'Unfortunate choice of words,' she said. 'The plan is to bring you up before Judge Joshua Harding when he arrives in town on next week's stage. Harding's the kind of judge who likes to hear the stretch of a rope round a man's neck, so I figure that you'll be staying round for a long, long time.'

'Joshua Harding,' Sam Limbo yelped, instantly off his food. 'That old bastard would hang a man for farting!'

'I can see that gentlemanly speech and' — she looked at the specks of food on his chin — 'eating habits are not your strongest points,' she snorted.

The shocking consequences of facing Judge Joshua Harding hitting home with hammer blow force, Sam Limbo said with quiet awe, 'I'm as good as dead.'

'That you are,' the woman said with, Limbo reckoned, callous indifference and matter-of-fact statement. 'Your food's getting cold.'

'You might say, *ma'am*,' he emphasized, 'that I've gone right off my grub. Seeing that in a short time from now, I won't need to eat at all.'

'Then you won't want lunch,' she said, with even greater indifference, turning heel.

'Who are you?' Limbo enquired. 'Satan's sister!'

'No,' she replied calmly. 'The marshal's daughter.'

'Same thing,' Limbo flung back.

She paused, and gave advice that Sam Limbo thought was about as useful as a bucket with a hole in it for carrying water.

'You should get some rest. Judge Harding likes men he's about to hang to look fresh and well rested.'

'I'll get all the rest I can take when he's done with me,' Limbo growled.

The marshal's daughter looked at

him critically, 'I'll talk to Pa about a visit to the tonsorial parlour. A haircut, bath and shave wouldn't go amiss.'

'Why bother? Jesus won't be troubled. He had a beard, too.'

'Jesus?' she chuckled. 'If you see Him at all, it will be a very brief meeting before He sends you packing, I reckon. 'Bye now.'

'I'm an innocent man,' he called after her.

'Sure you are,' she replied, unconvinced. 'Never knew a killer who wasn't.'

'I killed that card-sharp in a fair fight.'

'You murdered a citizen of this town, that's what you did,' the marhsal's daughter stated uncompromisingly. 'And for that you'll hang. It's called justice.'

The door of the law office shut behind her.

Sam Limbo collapsed on to the bunk. He had counted on, at most, a couple of days in jail, a restful hiatus of plentiful sleep and grub. Then the marshal would come round and see that he had killed the card cheat fairly and squarely, justice would be done, and he'd ride on to the next burg. Had he thought otherwise, he would not have accompanied the marshal as tamely as he had. 'Sam Limbo, sometimes you can be the dumbest critter in this whole wide West,' he groaned, holding his head in his hands.

Preoccupied with his woes, Sam Limbo was unaware that the marshal had entered the law office. 'Some gal, ain't she?' Andy Daly said, not asking a question but making a statement; a sentiment with which Sam Limbo wholeheartedly agreed. 'Every inch her ma's daughter.' Proudly wistful, he added, 'Rest Ellen's soul.'

He shook his head reflectively.

'When my wife died ten years ago, I never thought that I'd be able to fashion Sarah into the lady Ellen was. In fact, most times, when this town was getting on its feet and I had to deal with the kind of riff-raff that every new town has to deal with, she took care of herself and me, too, when I was trying to cope with Ellen's loss as well as tote a badge.'

A sadness filled Andy Daly's eyes.

'And now, with Sarah of marriageable age, it won't be long before she'll be gone too. I reckon that Nat Burnett will soon pop the question. That'll leave me an old warhorse with nothing much left to do but rock on the porch.'

The silence between the men lengthened. Sam Limbo, not normally given to listening to sob stories, had been deeply moved by Daly's sincerity. But if there were words he could have said, none came. Partly because of a hard life having coarsened his heart, he was not good at sympathizing, having missed out on the finer emotions of life, but mostly his silence was because of the shock of the marshal's news that Sarah Daly was about to become Mrs Nat Burnett, whoever the heck Nat Burnett was.

At first, why that should trouble him, he was not at all sure. But reflecting on his disappointment, Limbo realized that in some small corner of his mind a tiny seed of hope that he might become closer to Sarah Daly had been planted during her feisty visit. It was a crazy notion, which he now dismissed out of hand. He was a saddletramp! The next town always looked more hopeful. His days and nights were spent either on the trail, or in smoky saloons playing cards to get the money to saddle-up and ride on yet again — a nomadic life that no woman could settle to. And no man worth his salt should follow. But losing his mother and sister to an Indian attack when he was fifteen had made putting down roots again difficult for him; always fearful that if he got too close to any other soul, he'd lose them too. The couple of times he had tried to settle, the images of that sorrowful afternoon when the Apaches attacked their wagon haunted him, and he would once more find himself on another trail; one of an endless line of trails that he had always hoped would lead to at least contentment if not happiness. But as the years had gone by and it had never happened, Sam Limbo had come to accept that his life, long or short, would end under the stars or in some grimy saloon, the latter being the more likely. All of which, when he thought about it, made his ideas about somehow becoming cosy with Sarah Daly pretty ludicrous. And the sooner he dismissed the notion, the sooner he would become again the flint-hearted roamer he had been, right up to the second he had looked up and had seen Sarah holding breakfast.

'Got a wire,' Daly said. 'Judge Harding will be arriving early, day after tomorrow.'

The marshal's statement brought home to Sam Limbo the stark ridiculousness of harbouring a hope of jumping the gap between his kind of life and Sarah Daly's. In a couple of days he'd hang, if he was still in Dane's Bend. It did not matter that he would hang for a murder he did not commit.

The news of Harding's premature arrival in Dane's Bend meant that he had to set aside any silly thoughts and concentrate on busting out of jail, and that was all he needed to focus on.

'You know, of all the men I've seen hanged, you'll be the one I'll regret most, Limbo.'

'You know, Marshal,' Limbo said. 'That will be real nice knowing when that noose tightens round my neck.'

'You killed a man, Limbo,' the marshal said, his attitude hardening. 'And the penalty for murder is hanging.'

'Sure I killed a man,' Limbo conceded. 'Only I didn't murder him, Marshal. Archer was a cheat. I told him so. Gave him a chance to come clean. And whether you want to believe it or not, along with the aces up his sleeve he had a derringer. As plain a case of self-defence as could be.'

'That's your version, Limbo,' the badge-toter stated tersely. 'Like I told you. There was no derringer found. And that means in law there was no need for you to shoot Archer. And there ain't no witnesses either to speak up for you,' he added.

'That derringer was spirited away, Marshal. Don't you reckon that you have a clear duty to find it?' Marshal Andy Daly scowled darkly. 'And the only reason no one spoke up was that no one saw any merit in saving a saddlebum's neck from a noose.'

Before Sam Limbo could argue further, the door of the marshal's office burst open. A lanky specimen with whom Limbo had shared the blackjack table the previous night was breathless with the news he brought.

'Yancey Donovan's just ridden in, Marshal,' he announced. 'Bold as you like.'

'Yancey Donovan?' Daly checked. 'Are you sure, Frank?'

'Knowed him from that dodger that was goin' the rounds a coupla months back. He looks even meaner in the flesh.'

Clearly, Andy Daly was troubled by the messenger's news, and he was sensible to be worried, Limbo knew. Yancey Donovan was the youngest of four brothers whose infamy had spread far and wide. Another two men burst in to convey the same news.

'What're you going to do, Andy?' enquired the older of the well-dressed pair.

'Talk to him, Henry, I guess,' said Daly, lamely.

'Talk to him!' the second man of the duo exclaimed, his nature much brasher than his colleague. 'Talking won't do any good.'

'Andrew's right,' Henry said. 'Talking won't work with a man like Yancey Donovan.'

'You've got to run him out of town,' Andrew demanded.

Now Sarah Daly arrived in a rush, in time to hear the exchanges; exchanges that sent her into a fury. 'Don't talk horse manure, Mr Sloan,' she admonished the man who had just spoken.

'My pa's no match for the likes of Yancey Donovan.'

'He's the marshal, Sarah,' Andrew Sloan stated in a no-nonsense manner. 'It's his job. Plain and simple.'

'That'll be Miss Daly to you!' Sarah said.

Sloan's partner had his say.

'Andrew's right, *Miss* Daly. Your father is the law in Dane's Bend, and it's his sworn duty to see to it that the citizens of Dane's Bend don't come to any harm at the hands of a man like Yancey Donovan.'

'Hold it, Sarah,' said Daly when, even more furious, Sarah was ready to launch another broadside. 'Mr Sloan and Mr Wilkins are right, gal.'

'Yancey Donovan's in the saloon right now, Marshal,' Andrew Sloan said. 'I recommend that you should strike while the iron is hot.'

'Pa, if you face Yancey Donovan on your own, I reckon that I'll be putting you down with Ma tomorrow.' Sarah Daly swung round on the marshal's visitors. 'A man like Yancey Donovan is a town matter — '

'A town matter?' Andrew Sloan questioned. 'What do you mean by a town matter?'

Sarah said, 'I mean that when my pa faces Yancey Donovan, he'll not have to do it alone. That's what I mean by it being a town matter, Mr Sloan. Are you gents willing to stand with him?'

'Have you taken leave of your senses, young woman?' Henry Wilkins said. 'Andrew and I are bankers, not gunmen.'

'We pay town taxes that pays the marshal's wages,' Sloan said.

'The lady's got a point, gents.'

All eyes went to Sam Limbo.

'Who the hell asked you?' Sloan grumbled. 'Keep your danm nose out of our business, jail-bird!'

Sam Limbo settled his gaze on Andy Daly.

'You might as well cut your own throat right now if you're going up against Yancey Donovan, Marshal,' he said. 'Save you having to listen to all that loud noise from Donovan's blasting sixguns.'

'No one's giving me credit here,' Daly said, angrily. 'I've faced men like Yancey Donovan before, and I'm still standing.'

'When?' Limbo enquired.

'A couple of years ago. The McGrath twins.'

'The McGraths were raw amateurs compared to the Donovans,' Limbo said.

'Let Yancey Donovan be, Pa,' Sarah pleaded. 'He'll ride on. There's nothing here for him.'

'Let him be,' Sloan said, 'and word will get out. Soon the streets will be crawling with Donovan's kind.'

'Mr Sloan is right, Sarah,' Daly said. 'I'll order Donovan out of town right now.'

'Pa . . . '

'Don't fret so, Sarah,' the marshal told his daughter. 'You get along home now.'

The sound of an exploding gun rang over the town.

'Get going, Marshal,' Andrew Sloan demanded. 'Looks like you've dithered too long as it is.'

Grim-faced, Marshal Andy Daly shrugged off his daughter's restraining hand on his arm, and marched out of the law office.

'If my pa is killed by Yancey Donovan, I'll kill both of you,' she told Andrew Sloan and Henry Wilkins, and vowed, 'So help me God.'

'You know, fellas,' said Sam Limbo. 'If Marshal Daly catches lead, I figure you're walking dead men.'

Exchanging worried glances, the bankers hurried from the marshal's office. Sarah Daly buried her head in her hands and wept.

'Miss Sarah,' said Frank, the man who had first brought the news of Yancey Donovan's arrival in town. 'I think I've got a pretty good idea.'

'Idea?' Sarah asked hopefully. 'Well, then, speak up.'

The man looked to Sam Limbo. 'What if Mr Limbo backed your Pa's play.'

Sarah Daly's thoughtful gaze settled on Limbo.

'Forget it,' Limbo said. 'I ain't interested.'

'He's fast,' Frank told Sarah.

'You help my pa now, and I'll see to it that Judge Harding gets to know about it,' Sarah promised Limbo.

'Well, the thing is, if I agree to throw in with the marshal,' Limbo said. 'I might not be around to hang in a couple of days' time anyway.'

'So what have you got to lose?' Sarah argued. 'Get shot now, or hang later? Dead is dead. And there's a chance that Harding won't hang you if you've helped the law.'

Sam Limbo said, 'You sure have a way of cutting to the chase, Miss Daly.'

'I haven't got time to pussyfoot about, Mr Limbo.' Worry weighed Sarah Daly down. 'My pa should be arriving at the saloon right about now.

So what's it to be? Hang for certain in a couple of days? Or take a chance on dying now? And if you don't, maybe putting Judge Harding in a generous frame of mind.'

Sam Limbo's response was, 'Let me out of here.'

Sarah grabbed the keys from the marshal's desk and had the cell door open in a second. Then she hurried ahead of Limbo and had his gunbelt ready to buckle on when he reached the desk.

'I must be loco,' Limbo murmured.

Sarah Daly kissed him on the cheek.

'If this doesn't work out, I'd like a deck of cards to be put in my casket.'

'Deal,' she said. 'Go.' She shooed him out of the office.

'Has this mantrap got a back door?'

'Back door?'

'Yeah. Back door,' Limbo repeated.

Sarah led him to the back door of the jail.

'Mr Limbo . . . ' Sam Limbo paused as he hurried away. 'Don't try and flee.

If you do, I'll cut you down like a mangy dog.'

'Don't doubt it for a second, Sarah,' Limbo said, and continued on his way to the rear of the Thirsty Dog Saloon where, on arriving, he went up the external stairs and climbed through a window at the top which let him into a hallway from where he made his way to the stairs leading down into the saloon. Below, a man was sniggering: Yancey Donovan, he reckoned. He slipped out of his boots and crept down the stairs in his stockinged feet.

'Would you say that again, Marshal,' Yancey Donovan asked. ' 'Cause I reckon I didn't hear so good.'

'You heard,' Andy Daly said. 'Now, do it.'

'You want me to just drop my guns, right?' Yancey Donovan sneered. 'I don't figure I will, Marshal. So I guess if you want them, you're goin' to have to take them off me when I'm dead.' He laughed. 'Shit, you won't be able to do that, will ya? 'Cause, ya see, you'll be dead long before that.'

Yancey Donovan's killer's eyes bored into the marshal.

'Now, Marshal, you say you're sorry for upsettin' me and I just might let you walk outa here.'

'Hell will freeze over first, Donovan!' Andy Daly barked.

'In that case, make your play,' the hardcase flung back.

'Real sorry to break up the party,' Sam Limbo crooned, leaning over the banister, sixgun on Yancey Donovan as he swung round. 'Now, I figure that you should do as the marshal says, Donovan, or I'll just plug you 'tween the eyes.'

'That a fact?' Yancey Donovan put on a show of bravado, until he realized that Sam Limbo would do exactly what he had said he would. 'Do you know who I am?' he asked.

'Sure I do,' Limbo chuckled. 'Knew your pa well. Coyote's the name, ain't it. 'Cause that's what your pa was, a stinking coyote.'

Yancey Donovan dived for his gun. Sam Limbo's bullet lifted the hat off his head and tossed it in the air. Donovan's hand stalled.

'Now maybe I'll just put that bullet 'tween your eyes to show you that I can, huh?'

Yancey Donovan unbuckled his gun-belt.

'Obliged,' Sam Limbo said. 'Now, I figure that it's time you hit the trail, don't you?'

Yancey Donovan studied Sam Limbo.

'I won't forget you,' he said.

'Shucks, that's just what your sister said, too.'

'You're a dead man.'

'Git, Donovan,' Limbo ordered. 'You've worn out your welcome in this burg.'

Before disappearing through the batwings, with Sam Limbo directly behind him to make sure that he left town, Yancey Donovan repeated his threat.

'Figure the hangman will beat you to it, Donovan,' Limbo said.

'Hangman? Then why're you throwin' in your lot with the law?'

''Cause I reckon that I'm the dumbest critter who ever came down the line. Goodbye, Donovan. Hope you catch lead real soon.'

'Not before I deliver some into your gut, mister,' he growled.

* * *

Sarah Daly's tension turned to leg-weary relief when she saw Yancey Donovan come from the saloon and mount up, watched all the way by her pa and Sam Limbo. She grabbed hold of the man whose idea it was to enlist Limbo's help and danced him round the marshal's office.

'Donovan ain't rightly gone yet, ma'am,' Frank cautioned.

Of course he was right. Yancey Donovan was the kind of trailwise *hombre* who would have a bagful of tricks he could call on. Coming down to earth, Sarah anxiously returned to the window to check on Donovan's progress, and she was overjoyed to see him riding along the main street headed out of town. It was a sight that was mighty pleasing to the eye, but it was a joy that was immediately dimmed by the fact that the hope of a longterm partnership and friendship between her pa and Sam Limbo could not be. As soon as Donovan was gone, Sam would be back in jail and counting on Judge Harding taking a kinder view of him for helping the law in Dane's Bend. Sarah now felt guilty about having persuaded Sam to help her pa by holding out a hope of Harding judging him kindlier. The fact was that Joshua Harding was a merciless man who enforced the law to the letter, and seldom, if ever, took mitigating circumstances into account.

Sarah Daly's glum thoughts were interrupted by a man shouting in the street outside the marshal's office.

'Donovan, you murdering bastard, I'm going to blast you right into hell in a million pieces!'

She swung round to see a man called Harry Long, the owner of the livery, blocking Yancey Donovan's path. But what in tarnation was he doing, holding Donovan under the threat of a shotgun? Why the devil had he not just left well enough alone and let Yancey Donovan ride out of town? Her dancing partner had the answer.

'Donovan and his brothers rode with Quantrell in the war. That was bad enough, but on the day the war ended Donovan and his three brothers, each one more rotten that the other, rode into a town called Brown's Landing. Harry owned the livery there at that time. Harry was at the general store collecting a dress that had been freighted in for him from Boston for his wife's birthday. He had left his wife helping out at the livery until he got back.

'Well, I guess Harry Long's cursed that day ever since. Yancey Donovan and his brother Spence raped and then murdered Harry's wife. When he got back from the general store he found her, bloodied and defiled. But by then the Donovans had left town. Harry spent the next three years looking for them, before he got lung-sickness that prevented him from searching anymore.'

Yancey Donovan, sensing the terrible danger he was in, tried palaver as a means to extricate himself from a potentially deadly situation. 'Why, mister,' he crooned pleasantly, his face a mask of angelic innocence, 'I don't know why you're ranting so?' The stiletto was sliding down his sleeve. Any second it would be in the palm of his hand. 'But a man's got a right to know what it is he's accused of, don't you reckon?'

'Brown's Landing,' Long snarled. 'Remember Brown's Landing, Donovan?' He laughed insanely. 'The livery.'

Yancey Donovan shook his head. 'Can't say that I do, mister.'

The ivory handle of the stiletto was comfortingly cool in Yancey Donovan's palm. Another second or two and he would be ready to throw the knife and, as always, it would reach its target with deadly accuracy.

'A blonde woman at the livery,' Harry Long prompted. 'Real pretty.'

The stiletto ready, Yancey Donovan scoffed, 'Yeah. I recall now.' He sneered. 'Ya know, mister, that woman wasn't near as pleasing as me and my brother Spence reckoned she would be.'

Harry Long squeezed the triggers of the shotgun at the same instant the stiletto stuck in his windpipe. But Yancey Donovan's horse, which he had stolen in another town a couple of days before, was not used to the outlaw's ways and bucked at the last second into the buckshot released by Long's jerking finger. Most of the shotgun's load missed Yancey Donovan, but the little that hit him was enough to take the side of his head away.

Donovan crashed to the street to lie alongside Harry Long. The roar of the shotgun lifted over the town like the angry roar of a departing demon.

Sarah Daly staggered back from the window of the marshal's office, pale and weak, because she knew the import of what had happened. Trouble that had been riding out of Dane's Bend only a moment before, would now return with a vengence.

On the saloon porch, Marshal Andy Daly was expressing the same opinion to Sam Limbo.

3

Sarah watched uneasily as the marshal slammed the cell door shut on Sam.

'Nothing I can do, Sarah,' he said. 'There's still a charge of murder to be answered.'

'Sam's just saved your hide,' she argued hotly.

'Sam?' Daly barked.

'Sam,' she stated defiantly. 'Now, like I was saying — '

He addressed Limbo. 'To you, Limbo, my daughter is Miss Daly and off limits. And you save your breath, Sarah! Limbo stays put. And you had no right to make him any promises.'

'You'd be in the undertaker's right now, if Sam had not stepped in,' Sarah said. 'There was no way that you'd've beaten Yancey Donovan to the draw.'

'I didn't need to. I was toting a blaster.'

'Even so, you might still be in the funeral parlour.' She held her father's gaze. 'No one else around here helped.'

'And I didn't ask for anyone's help,' Daly growled. 'So you had no right to look for it, Sarah.'

'You're a mule stubborn man, Andy Daly,' Sarah rebuked her father. 'And you've got the kind of pride that saw Satan fall from heaven like lightning, too.'

Sarah turned to Sam.

'I lied, Sam,' she said. 'I could plead with Judge Harding till my lungs give out, but he'll still hang you. Harding is a hanging judge.'

'I knew that, Sarah,' he said. 'Harding is a burned-out old reprobate who can only now get pleasure from sending men to the gallows.'

'Don't you have chores to do at home?' Daly quizzed his daughter. And, not waiting for an answer, added, 'Well, go and do them, Sarah.'

Sarah Daly was of a mind to continue the argument with her father, but

Limbo said that it would be best to end the dispute.

'I want you on the next stage out of town to Larksville, young lady,' Daly said. 'It's been a long while since you visited with your aunt Lucy.'

'That's because Aunt Lucy and me rub together like a match to a fuse,' Sarah complained.

'Don't argue. You're on your way to your aunt Lucy's and that's an end of it, Sarah.'

Sarah Daly stormed out, muttering under her breath.

Andy Daly threw himself on to the chair behind his desk and sighed, heavy-shouldered.

'My advice, Marshal,' Limbo said, after a long silence, 'is to swear in a half-dozen deputies toting shotguns.'

'Did I ask for your advice?' Daly growled.

'Have sense, Marshal. When those Donovan boys ride in here, which they most assuredly will when news reaches them about their brother, you'd better have a reception committee waiting to greet them.'

'It could take months for the Donovan outfit to get news of Yancey's demise.'

'Days, weeks, months or years, it don't matter. When they do, they'll head this way with only one thought in mind: and that will be to take as much revenge for Yancey's death as they can take. And I reckon that the Donovans, being as close as peas in a pod since they were kids, ain't that far away, Marshal.'

'Nice of you to worry about me, Limbo,' said Daly sarcastically.

Sam Limbo chuckled. 'I don't give a hang if the Donovans carve you up and feed you to the dogs, Daly. But I know what they do to women they take a shine to. And Sarah is a woman any man would take a shine to.'

'Don't you think I know that, Limbo? That's why Sarah will be on the stage out of here.'

'And if the Donovans get here before

the stage? Yancey Donovan scouts the territory that the outfit is interested in before they move on it. Therefore, I reckon, that's what Yancey was doing in Dane's Bend.'

'What the hell is there to interest desperadoes like the Donovans in this one-horse burg, Limbo?'

'On the face of it, not much,' Sam Limbo conceded, 'but the Donovan brothers don't waste their time, that I do know.'

The marshal's interest in Sam Limbo became keener. 'You seem to know a hell of a lot about the Donovan outfit, Limbo.' His interest became even keener still. 'A man of your drifting ways might be a fellow-traveller of an outfit such as the Donovans. Maybe you were Yancey Donovan's interest in this burg, Limbo.'

'That's loco thinking, Daly. Would I help put the run under Yancey Donovan if that was so?'

'You could be a real clever *hombre*, Limbo.' Daly stood up and came to face Sam Limbo in his cell. 'Maybe you played a canny hand by showing yourself. That way you let Donovan know that you were here. And Harry Long, stepping out with a blaster, was just the kind of fly in the ointment that sends the best laid plans awry.'

'You're forgetting that it was Sarah who asked me to step in, Daly. I never said a word about helping you.'

'You're a clever fella, I reckon, Limbo. The kind of man who can get folk to do what he wants them to do without them even knowing they're doing it. A nudge here, a nod there. A word here, a word there. And before you know it, your listener believes that they're doing it all of their own free will.'

Sam Limbo laughed.

'I'd like to think that I'm half as smart as you give me credit for, Daly,' he said. 'But the fact is, you're talking one hundred per cent horseshit!' He settled an unwavering gaze on the Dane's Bend marshal. 'You're scared,

Marshal, and that's nothing to be ashamed of. You'd have to have a hole in your head not to be.

'Sure I've crossed paths with the Donovans, mean murdering bastards one and all — an outfit that I'd rather sup with the devil than kow-tow to. What I did on Sarah's asking was done for her. Believe it or shove it up your . . .

'Well, that's the way it was and is.'

Andy Daly's anger faded away.

'You're right, Limbo. I'm no match for hard-cases like the Donovans,' he admitted. 'For everyday law and order in this burg, I get by. Nothing much more than cracking heads together on a rowdy Saturday night. Stepping in when a coupla fellas take a fancy to the same gal. That kind of thing. But nothing in the league of trouble that the Donovans could visit on us.'

'You handled me pretty slickly,' Limbo said.

'You were at the end of a shotgun.' He sighed deeply. 'The trouble with a blaster is that once you've pulled the triggers it's about as useless as a eunuch in a brothel. A shotgun would dispatch one Donovan to the devil. But . . . '

The marshal shook his head hopelessly.

Sam Limbo knew that he should be over the moon about the marshal's troubles, because the more trouble that was heaped on his plate, the greater the chance would be for him to avoid a hangman's rope. However, strangely, he found a kinship with the man. His pa had been a lawman, pretty much in Andy Daly's mould, capable and honest, but no fast-draw badge-toter. The situation on the day he died in a burg called Lotts Gap mirrored what was happening right now in Dane's Bend. A drunken brawl. Hasty gunfire. A man who had kin of a revengeful nature caught lead. If Abe Limbo had had any sense he'd have handed in his badge there and then, but like Andy Daly, he would not dishonour it by turning tail. And he also reckoned that because of that honour, Daly would end up like his pa: dead and quickly forgotten by the folk and town he'd tried to defend.

'You could always take that star off your chest, Marshal,' he suggested.

Daly looked with a raking contempt at Limbo, as if he was something that he might have found on the sole of his boot.

'If I did that,' he growled, 'I'd have had no right to wear it in the first place. The West needs law and order badly to rid it of scum like the Donovans. And it won't get it by badge-toters turning tail, Limbo!'

The words might have come from his own pa's mouth.

'Then you'd best round up those deputies you'll need,' Limbo advised.

'Deputies,' he scoffed despairingly. 'Even if I could get the men to deputize, they'd likely not be able to hit the side of a barn at ten paces after taking aim for half an hour. Dane's

Bend is a trading town, Limbo, not some border hell-hole where a man learns quickly to shoot fast and straight or dies.'

'You've got a real mountain to climb, ain't you?' Sam Limbo observed.

The door of the marshal's office opened and Henry Wilkins burst in. The sudden interruption had the marshal swinging about, his hand diving for his sixgun.

'Damn and tarnation, Mr Wilkins,' Daly rebuked the flustered man. 'Don't you know better than to come barging in when the atmosphere is crackling?'

Andrew Stone quickly followed on Wilkins's heels, every bit as concerned.

'Henry and I don't have time for the niceties, Marshal,' Andrew Sloan barked. 'I'll come straight to the point: what do you intend doing about the Donovan gang?'

'Do?' Daly yelped. 'Who says that there'll be anything that needs doing, Mr Sloan?'

'Don't bury your head in the sand

until someone shoots you in the ass,' Sloan said. 'That fool Harry Long killed Yancey Donovan, and by so doing he has put Dane's Bend in the Donovans' sights. You should have anticipated what Long's reaction to Yancey Donovan would be, Daly, after what they did to his wife.'

'I didn't know Harry was in town,' Daly said. 'He must have got back early from that horse fair over in Santon Falls.'

Andrew Sloan spoke again.

'I think we can take it as read that the Donovan brothers will want to avenge their dead brother. But as the town bankers, Henry and I have another problem. Tell the marshal, Henry.'

'Two days ago, the bank took possession of a fortune of two hundred thousand dollars and as much again in bonds, the property of a very rich Mexican who feels that his riches are less safe in Mexico with so much peasant unrest there.'

The news staggered the marshal, and

brought a low whistle from Sam Limbo. Now they knew why Yancey Donovan had come to town. His task had obviously been to reconnoitre Dane's Bend. Also to gauge the mettle of the marshal and the townfolk, to plan for any resistance they might meet. Had he had the opportunity to report back to his brothers, Limbo reckoned that they would be happy men with what Yancey would have had to report.

Andrew Sloan set aside Henry Wilkins's timid stating of the bank's case. 'The marshal doesn't need a history lesson, Henry.' He addressed Daly in the same brisk manner. 'Obviously the Donovans got wind of the lodgement, and plan to rob the bank. And what we want to know' — he waved his hand to include Henry — 'is how you're going to prevent that happening, Marshal?

'Well?' he demanded in seconds, when Andy Daly's plan did not materialize.

'Plans take time to plan,' the marshal

said lamely. 'Like I've been telling Mr Limbo here, this is a trading town, sadly short of gun-handy men.'

Andrew Sloan shot Limbo a contemptuous glance.

'Talking to a man waiting for a gallows trap door to spring open, was really stupid, Marshal,' he stated bluntly. 'A man of his kind could be hand in glove with the Donovans.'

'He helped the marshal, Andrew,' Henry Wilkins pointed out, clearly ill at ease with Sloan's brash approach.

'What does that prove?' Sloan barked, more and more annoyed by Wilkins's gentlemanly attitude. 'Didn't either of you think that the whole point of murdering Benjamin Archer was to place himself right at the centre of things here in town? Like he is right now, the enemy within? There was never any threat to his neck. When the Donovans rode in, he'd be as free as a bird.'

Though it was untrue, it was obvious that the banker's theory had renewed Daly's suspicions of him, and Sam saw no point in denying the allegation because he reckoned that the mountain of Daly's suspicion would be too difficult to overcome.

'So,' Sloan settled waspish eyes on Sam, 'maybe we should have the sense to steal their thunder by hanging this man right now.'

'Without a fair trial?' the marshal protested.

'He shot Archer down in cold blood, didn't he?' the banker challenged Daly. 'All a trial will do is reach the same conclusion and hang him. He'll be one less snake in the grass to worry about when the Donovans arrive. So I say, sling a rope now and be done with it.'

'There'll be no lynching in my town,' Andy Daly stated tersely.

'Are you defending this man, Marshal Daly?' Henry Wilkins questioned, bemused.

'No, sir,' the marshal responded. 'Once Judge Harding has sentenced Limbo to hang — which he will — I'll sling the rope myself.'

'Meanwhile we have to take the risk of having a Donovan cohort in our midst,' Sloan stated.

Sam Limbo figured that it was time to speak up.

'I wouldn't spit on any Donovan,' he said, 'because I figure it would be a waste of good spit.'

'So you say,' Andrew Sloan flung back. 'But what man in his right senses' — his glance went to Daly — 'would believe you, Limbo? If the bank is raided, I'll see to it that you'll answer for it, Marshal. Meanwhile, Henry,' he said as he turned to leave, 'I think it would be wise for you and I to hire our own security.'

'I'll not tolerate a private army in town,' Daly blustered.

'I don't see that we have any choice, Marshal Daly,' Wilkins said. 'Andrew and I just can't stand idly by and let the Donovans rob our bank.'

'Come, Henry,' Sloan commanded his partner. 'Time talking to the marshal is time wasted.'

carrying, scattering the contents of lunch across the floor. 'You should have stayed in the house,' he rebuked her.

'What's going on, Pa? The town's a powder keg.'

The marshal quickly filled her in on the dramatic events which had unfolded since she had left, and Sarah Daly immediately understood the possible consequences of the bankers' recruitment drive.

'All hell could break loose,' she stated, starkly.

'That's why I want you off the streets and indoors, Sarah,' the marshal said.

'You'll need me here: I can shoot pretty straight.'

'Go home, Sarah,' Daly ordered. And then, softly, 'I couldn't stand it if anything happened to you, honey.'

He laughed reflectively.

'And your ma would come down from Heaven and skin me alive, if it did.'

'You need help,' Sarah said, keenly concerned. She looked to Limbo. 'Will

The bankers marched out of the marshal's office.

'Looks like this burg's problems are growing by the second, Marshal,' Sam Limbo observed, and added wryly, 'in future I'll have to be more choosy about the towns I visit.'

'You don't have a future, Limbo,' the Dane's Bend lawman snarled.

4

'You'll wear out that floor if you keep pacing like that,' Limbo said, an hour after the bankers had departed, a time during which Andy Daly had spent going from his desk to the window to check on the entrances to the town, and also to keep an eye on developments in the saloon where Sloan had made tracks to, and to where, shortly after, men had begun arriving — more and more men. 'Can't blame them, Marshal. What I've seen of Dane's Bend it's going through a rough patch. Money in a man's pocket is scarce. And those bankers have lots of cash to buy what they want.'

'Don't they realize how stupid they're being?' Daly wailed. 'By now the whole darn town must know about the riches in the bank. They could be stoking up more trouble in town than they'd ever

get from the Donovans.'

The point Daly had made was a valid one. In his travels, Sam Limbo had seen towns where guns had been hired out for one reason or another, and in most cases it had turned ugly. And the saloon in any town was the worst place to recruit. Liquor and guns were a fatal combination. All it needed was for one dispute to erupt (and every town had its combative elements) and the mixture of whiskey and lead soon came into play. And once the shooting began, all reason flew out the window, and old scores were settled. And by the time the trouble they were hired to counter arrived in town, all that needed to be done was for the visitors to mop up the remains of what had been intended to be the resistance.

'Damn it!' Daly swore, craning his neck to look along the street. He hurried to the door and yanked it open. 'Get inside, Sarah,' he ordered, and hurried his daughter into the law office, causing her to drop the basket she wa

you help again, Sam?'

'There's no need,' the marshal growled. 'I'll go and talk to the men in the saloon. Set them straight on how badly this whole thing might turn out. I know each and every man, Sarah. They'll listen to me.'

Their attention was got by rowdy shouting. Daly and Sarah went to the window. Two men were stumbling out of the saloon, sharing slugs from a bottle of rotgut.

'Damn Andrew Sloan!' Daly swore.

'Where are you going?' Sarah fretted, as the marshal headed for the door.

'To nip this madness in the bud, that's where.'

'I wouldn't go out there right now, Marshal,' was Sam Limbo's advice.

'You keep your counsel to yourself, Limbo,' Daly barked, and strode from the office, shrugging off Sarah's restraining hand.

The two drunks saw the lawman come across the street.

'Howdy, Marshal,' one of the men

greeted him affably, holding out the bottle of rotgut. 'Have a drink.'

Andy Daly grabbed the bottle and slung it down an alley. 'Go home and sleep it off, Charlie. Mary ain't well, and she'll be worried.'

'Heh!' the second man shouted aggressively. 'You ain't got no right to do that, Marshal.'

On seeing the man's reaction to her father's action, Sarah let out a little whimper of fear.

'You go on home, too, Ed,' Daly ordered sternly.

'And if I don't wanna?' Ed challenged. 'How're ya goin' to make me, badge-toter?'

Without hesitation, Daly swung a fist to Ed's jaw that catapulted him backwards. He got dizzily to his feet, but when the bells ceased clanging inside his head his aggression reached new heights.

'Leave it be, Ed,' Charlie said, having sobered considerably. 'Andy's right. We should both be at home. We've got families to think about.' When it looked like Charlie's plea was going to fall on deaf ears, he said, 'We ain't town trash, Ed.'

'Guess not,' Ed said. 'Sorry, Andy.'

'Thanks, fellas,' said the marshal as they walked away.

Spent with tension, Sarah Daly leaned against the wall for support.

'Looks like the marshal talked sense into those fellas, huh?' Limbo observed.

'It was touch and go, Sam. For a moment it could have gone either way.'

Another man came to the batwings of the saloon and hailed the men walking away. 'Where're you fellas headed?'

'Home,' Ed said.

The man's gaze went to the marshal. 'On your orders, Marshal?'

'What's happening now?' Limbo enquired, on seeing Sarah Daly's tension return full blown.

'Ace Danagher's put in a show,' she replied breathlessly. 'A hardcase, if ever there was one.'

'Trouble for the marshal?'

Sarah nodded. 'I reckon, Sam. Danagher's got more than one crow to pluck. Pa's thrown him in jail a couple of times, and only a month ago he laid into him for lewd behaviour in front of Miss Quinn, our schoolteacher. Sober, he's mean and ornery; now, with whiskey sloshing in his belly, there's no telling where he'll draw the line.'

Across the street at the saloon, Andy Daly knew that Ace Danagher would bring a note of devilment to proceedings which he had hoped he'd be able to steer away from the potential mayhem fostered by makeshift law. However, now that the chief trouble-stirrer in Dane's Bend had got involved, the marshal knew that his task of reasoning with the men in the saloon, stoked by Ace Danagher's considerably persuasive lingo, was a task probably beyond his powers.

'The marshal asked and we're doin', Ace,' Ed said.

'Runnin' scared, huh?' Danagher sneered.

'I ain't scared, Danagher,' Ed bellowed. 'Of you or no man.'

'Don't look like that to me. Runnin' home to hide behind your wives' skirts, as you are.'

Ed turned and headed back, fists balled.

Daly stepped in front of him.

'Don't let Danagher get under your skin, Ed,' he counselled. 'His opinion ain't worth spit.'

'I'll go, Marshal,' Ed said. 'But I damn well won't forget.'

As Ed and Charlie walked away, Ace Danagher cut loose with clucking sounds.

'Cut it out, Danagher!' the marshal warned. 'If you don't want to end up in my jail.'

Danagher's reply was a mocking one. 'Why, Marshal Daly, if that happened, maybe I could get out to help you like Limbo did when them Donovan boys ride in.'

Marshal Andy Daly bristled.

'Danagher,' he said grimly, 'seeing

that you only blew into town a couple of months ago, I think it would be best if you blew out again come tomorrow.'

Ace Danagher chuckled and leaned against a support beam of the saloon porch overhang. He took the makings from his vest pocket, rolled a smoke and took a long deep drag of the weed. Then he said, 'You figuring on runnin' me outa town, Marshal?'

'If I have to,' the lawman stated.

Danagher took another drag of the weed, straightened up, and flicked the smoke over the marshal's head into the street. Andy Daly wisely ignored Danagher's action, intended no doubt to provoke a response which would justify Danagher's subsequent reaction. The marshal climbed the steps to the saloon. Danagher hurried ahead to hold the batwings open mockingly for him to pass inside. The Dane's Bend lawman's fists clenched to knock the mocking sneer off Danagher's face, but he swallowed his pride. Judging by the rowdiness of the men crowding the saloon, trouble would come to him. He would not have to seek it out.

Back in the marshal's office Sarah Daly relaxed a little, but she knew that the danger to her father was far from over. In fact it had probably not yet begun.

'Another hurdle over?' Sam Limbo enquired.

'A hundred more to come,' she said, fearfully. 'Pa's a good man, Sam. Fair, too. But goodness and fairness don't count for anything with the likes of Ace Danagher.'

'Seems like a real desperado,' Limbo observed. 'How come this fella Danagher's hanging round a no-consequence burg like Dane's Bend?'

'A no-consequence burg!' Sarah flared. 'Is that so, Mr Limbo?'

'Keep that pretty hair of yours on, Sarah,' Limbo said. 'You can't claim that Dane's Bend is jumping like a flea, can you?'

'Easy pickings,' Sarah stated bitterly. 'That's what holds Ace Danagher rooted.'

'What I've seen of the town, there ain't no pickings at all, Sarah.'

'There's always someone eager and ready to hire a man like Danagher, Sam.'

'Fast, is he?'

'No one's really sure. Everyone assumes that he is, so he's had a challenge free time, so far.'

When Andy Daly entered the saloon, Andrew Sloan was at the bar, one-shot glasses lined up along the bartop, the keeper going its length, pouring.

'Line them up again,' he ordered, when all the glasses were grabbed.

'Mr Sloan.'

The banker turned at the marshal's summons. 'Marshal,' he beamed. 'Come to join the party?'

'We need to talk,' Daly said.

'Talk?' Sloan asked vaguely. 'I don't think that we have anything to talk about, Marshal Daly.'

'I figure we do.' Daly pointed to a table out of the way in a far corner. 'Let's parley over there.'

'I'm very busy right now, Marshal. Perhaps later.'

'Now, damn it!' Daly barked.

'Now, Marshal, you really should watch your blood pressure,' the banker said, unfazed by the lawman's demand. 'The drinks are on me, everyone,' he shouted, before following Daly to the out of the way table where, seated, he demanded to know, 'Now what's all this about?'

'You're stoking big trouble for yourself,' the marshal advised the banker. 'Liquor and lead don't mix well, Mr Sloan.'

'You can't protect the bank's assets, Marshal,' the banker stated bluntly, 'so I've got to do something.'

'You think the bank's assets will be protected by raising a drunken mob?'

'What do you suggest I do, Marshal?' Sloan looked at the crowd of men hogging the bar, arms reaching over those already at the bar, trying to grab the free whiskey. 'Let the Donovans walk straight into the bank and rob it?'

'Does Henry Wilkins agree with what you're doing?'

'He hasn't said he doesn't, Marshal.'

'Well, I sure as hell don't. And I'm ordering you to stop right now, Sloan!'

'Look, Marshal, let's be honest. No man is going to risk his life for a couple of lousy dollars by pinning on a badge. And, if you'll excuse my bluntness, you had to have help handling Yancey Donovan. So what hope do you have of taming the Donovan brothers collectively, if you can't tame one?'

'Getting Limbo to help was Sarah's idea, not mine.'

'Well, all I can say is, that if Sarah persuaded your prisoner to come to your assistance she has a whole lot more sense that her father has. Yancey Donovan would have killed you, Marshal. Plain and simple.'

Though Andrew Sloan's dressing down was as bitter as gall to swallow, Andy Daly had to admit to himself — he'd be damned if he'd admit the same to Sloan — that the banker had a very strong case to make.

Now that he had delivered his broadside, Sloan's attitude became more placatory. 'Look, Andy, there's no shame for you in my rounding up private security for the bank, everyone understands that. Though you've served this town well and honestly, you just haven't got the skills to deal with a threat like the Donovan outfit. Few lawmen have. That's why they've pretty much ruled the roost around these parts and much further afield, too.

'So why don't you go home with that pretty daughter of yours and lie low until all of this blows over.'

The banker had made the mistake of overplaying his hand, dishing out more humble pie than Andy Daly could swallow in one helping.

'I'm the law in this burg, Sloan,' he grated. 'And as the marshal, I'm telling you fair and square right now that I'll not tolerate any private mob enforcing their will in my town.' Daly sprang out of his chair. 'Is that understood?'

Andrew Sloan was unfazed by the marshal's prickly response to his advice. His smile was one of benevolent indulgence for a fool. 'And what, Marshal, are you going to do about it?' he enquired smugly. He looked to the men milling round the bar. 'Free whiskey and ten dollars a day is hard to beat.'

'You want me to keep pourin', Mr Sloan?' the barkeep enquired, interpreting the banker's glance towards the bar as a possible curtailment of the free booze that had been flowing for most of an hour now.

'Keep pouring, Fred,' Sloan instructed the barkeep.

A loud cheer went up.

'Sure, Mr Sloan,' said the barkeep, beginning another round of filling the glasses lined up along the length of the bar.

'You're free to join us, if you like, Marshal,' Sloan invited.

'I'd rather sup with Satan, Sloan,' the Dane's Bend lawman growled. 'I just hope that you won't reap what you're sowing.'

Andrew Sloan's gaze went to Ace Danagher who was standing just inside the batwings, smirking cockily.

'Mr Danagher is my insurance, Marshal,' the banker said. 'He's on twenty dollars a day to see that those on ten don't get notions that might be to my disadvantage.' The banker strolled off to join the riff-raff at the bar; men whom he'd not have given the time of day to an hour before.

Smarting, Andy Daly left the saloon and made his way pacily to Henry Wilkins's house at the far end of the main street. Watching from the marshal's office, Sarah took her father's visit to the bank president's home as a sign of his failure to talk sense to Andrew Sloan, which hiked her worry to new heights. Daly's knock on the brass knocker of the Wilkins house was thunderous. The door was opened immediately, as if Andrew Sloan's banking partner was waiting for the marshal's visit.

‘Come in, Andy,’ Wilkins invited. ‘I’ve been expecting you.’

Wilkins showed the marshal into the sitting-room, Daly enquiring as he did, ‘Do you back this madness that Sloan is up to, Henry?’

The president of the Dane’s Bend bank turned to face the marshal. ‘Of course I don’t.’

‘Didn’t reckon that you would. So when are you going to rein Sloan in, Henry?’

Henry Wilkins’s face was a bleak landscape of worry. ‘It isn’t that straightforward.’

‘Why not? You’re the bank president. Sloan is only the vice president. I’ve just come from the saloon where he’s plying the town riff-raff with free whiskey. And Sloan’s not in a listening mood, Henry.’

‘I’m sure if you state your position strongly enough, Andrew will not want to disobey the law.’

‘Dammit, Henry. Take your head out of the sand, man. We’re facing a drunken mob on the streets toting guns. The Lord alone knows where that might end.'

'The bank has the right to protect its assets, Andy. You must see that. And if you can't do it, what choice is there?'

'I don't deny that right,' Daly conceded. 'But the way to do that is by lawful means, not by letting vigilantes loose on the street.'

Henry Wilkins slumped into an armchair, and the news he conveyed to the marshal was stunning. 'The fact is, Andy, I can't order Andrew to do anything.'

'Can't? Or won't?'

'Can't,' Wilkins confirmed. 'Because Andrew is the bank's prime shareholder.'

'How can that be, Henry?' the marshal questioned the banker. 'You started the bank. Sloan only came in a couple of years ago.'

'Simple,' said Henry Wilkins resignedly. 'Some of my investements weren't good — in fact they were downright bad. That made me a poorer man, which meant that Sloan, whose investments were top class became the richer and agreed to bail me out in return for a greater share of bank stock. The overall effect of which made Sloan the real president of the bank. Only we agreed that my name should remain on the door. Sloan's reasoning being that if there was even the slightest hint of trouble brewing at the bank, there could have been a run on it. He was right, of course. Which leaves me, in effect, the junior partner.'

So stunned was Andy Daly that he also sought the support of an armchair.

'That sure explains a whole lot, Henry,' he murmured.

'I tried to talk sense to Sloan,' Wilkins said, 'but he threatened to reveal the true state of affairs at the bank and pull out.'

'There's a strong argument in favour of being rid of such a snake, Henry,' the marshal counselled.

Henry Wilkins held Andy Daly's

gaze, an ocean of fear in the banker's eyes. 'If Sloan pulled out he'd take his assets with him, Andy. That would leave me way short of what I'd need to meet the bank's commitments, should there be a run on it. And, of course, it would leave me penniless.'

Wilkins sighed wearily.

'Now do you understand why I'm helpless to rein in Sloan?'

Marshal Andy Daly's last hope of avoiding the trouble ahead vanished.

On seeing him come from Henry Wilkins's house, Sarah Daly knew by her father's downcast gait that his worries had not eased. They had in fact increased, as did hers.

Sam Limbo felt a keen sense of pity for Sarah Daly. However, facing the hangman as he was, his only concern had to be getting out of jail and out of Dane's Bend before Judge Joshua Harding strung him up. So any trouble in town that would preoccupy the marshal, was trouble that could be to his advantage. But

Sam Limbo wondered why that prospect did not fill him with the joy it should have. And, when he thought about it, the answer was a simple one: Sarah Daly.

5

'Well, Pa,' Sarah said with a false cheeriness when the marshal entered the law office. 'Everything sorted out?'

'Sure,' he said, with equal false cheeriness. Passing by on his way to his desk, Andy Daly's clouded face told Sam Limbo a completely different story. He sank into his chair. 'The boys in the saloon are talking a lot of hot air, the kind a man spouts with a bellyful of rotgut. They'll be breaking up and wandering off home soon.'

'Great!' Sarah enthused. But try as she might to go along with her father's yarn, tears sprang to her eyes and spilled down her cheeks. 'What the heck are we dancing a darn jig for, Pa?' she railed. 'Unless it's practice for dancing on your grave?'

'What nonsense are you spouting, Sarah?' Daly said, still keeping up the pretence which his daughter had abandoned. 'You'll have rheumatism of the joints long before you'll be dancing on my grave, gal.'

'Oh, Pa,' she wailed. 'You're not fooling anyone. Those men in the saloon will soon be on the streets; Andrew Sloan's lackeys to protect Andrew Sloan's assets by fair means or foul.'

'You're reading it all wrong, Sarah,' Daly said, trying to the end to prevent her fretting.

Sarah Daly's fist slammed down on the marshal's desk. 'No, I'm not! I'm no fool, so don't treat me like one!'

Marshal Andy Daly's show of bravado collapsed.

'The situation's dire, isn't it?'

'The worst it could be,' Daly admitted.

'What had Henry Wilkins to say for himself? Allowing Sloan to stir trouble the way he's doing. I must say that Mr Wilkins's part in all of this puzzles me.'

'Henry's hands are tied, Sarah.' He

stymied her next question. 'That's all I can say. What Henry told me, he told me in confidence, and I'm not going to break that confidence, Daughter.'

Sarah Daly looked at Sam Limbo, her glance one of pleading, to which his response remained stictly neutral. But Sarah went ahead anyway.

'Sam helped once before, Pa, maybe — '

'Forget it, Sarah,' the marshal snapped. 'Limbo's a murderer, and that's an end of it. We can't have killers helping the law, can we?'

'I ain't a killer, Marshal,' Sam Limbo tersely reminded the Dane's Bend lawman.

'That's for a judge and jury to decide, once I place the evidence in front of them, Limbo.'

'Did you look for the derringer Archer had?'

'I did. There's no sign.'

'I saw the damn thing fly out of his hand, Marshal,' Limbo growled. 'I reckon you ain't tried hard enough.'

Marshal Andy Daly leaped out of his

chair and stormed to the cells to come face to face with his prisoner. 'I gave it my best and most honest shot,' he declared. 'No one is saying they saw a derringer except you, Limbo. And in my book that don't count for much, seeing that you're facing a gallows.'

His face became pure stone.

'Witnesses swear that you gunned Archer down in cold blood, for no good reason other than he pulled an ace from up his sleeve.'

'A cheat always risks getting killed, Marshal,' Sam Limbo said, and stated with more than a modicum of truth, 'Archer wouldn't be the first card sharp to catch lead.'

'In my book and in my town, killing a man over a game of cards can't be justified,' Daly stated uncompromisingly.

'Pa, the whole town knows that Archer was a card cheat. Folk said that he couldn't help himself. Something in him made him cheat.'

Andy Daly conceded his daughter's argument, but he was unrelenting in his determination to put Sam Limbo on trial. 'Limbo stays behind bars, Sarah. And I don't want to hear another word about him helping me. Is that clear?'

'You're being a stubborn old war-horse,' Sarah declared. 'And when your mule-headedness gets you killed, do you think this godforsaken town will care a fig?'

Andy Daly's anger was replaced by a sad reflectiveness.

'I learned a long time ago that a man would be a fool to pin on a star, Sarah,' he said, 'if it was thanks he was expecting. A man wears a star in the hope that he can make this country a better and safer place to live in.'

'That'll do nicely on your tombstone, Pa,' Sarah said, equally saddened.

* * *

Rob Donovan, the oldest of the four Donovan brothers, checked his solid gold pocket watch (stolen from a man he had shot down without due cause a couple of weeks previously) and frowned.

'Dang it, Rob,' groaned Spence Donovan, the next eldest of the brothers sharing a fire, 'You'll have the gold on that watch worn away, slidin' it in and outa your pocket all the time.'

Art Donovan backed his brother's observation.

'Spence is right, Rob. A man shouldn't check the time too often, just in case he finds out that it's run out.'

Rob Donovan shoved the gold timepiece back into his vest pocket. 'Yancey's been gone a long time, Brothers. Ain't you concerned?'

'Yancey's full of spit, Rob.' Spence Donovan sighed. 'I bet right now he's beddin' a dove. Lucky bastard. Wish I had me a woman right now.'

'Me, too,' Art Donovan groaned. 'I gotta real bad yearnin', fellas.'

'Even if he dallied, Yancey should be back,' Rob Donovan said. 'Dane's Bend ain't the other end of the world. He's been gone way too long. I figure we should saddle up and go see what's keepin' our little brother, Brothers.'

'I ain't in no humour to set out this late,' Spence Donovan said.

'I ain't 'xactly bustin' to hit the saddle m'self, Rob,' Art joined in. 'Now a coupla hours' shuteye and I'd be rarin' to go.'

'And what if Yancey's in trouble?' Rob Donovan challenged his brothers.

Spence chuckled. 'In Dane's Bend, Rob?'

'Yeah,' Art said. 'Dane's Bend is a one-horse burg. Nothin' or no one there to worry our little brother.'

'Don't be so sure,' Rob Donovan rasped. 'It's often in a no-consequence burg like Dane's Bend that a surprise is thrown up. It was in a backwater like it that your uncle Ben got gutshot.'

'Uncle Ben was bushwhacked by a shooter in a dark alley, Rob,' Art Donovan reminded his older brother.

Rob Donovan cast a mean eye Art's way. 'Every town's got alleys. And it don't matter how you catch lead, you're still dead.'

Spence and Art Donovan had a moment's worry, before Spence said, 'Uncle Ben was pretty dumb, Rob. Yancey ain't. He's got Ma's instead of Pa's brains.'

Not wanting to push his brothers into an argument and generate days of ill will between them, Rob Donovan relented.

'We ride first light. I just hope that if Yancey's in trouble we won't be too late.' He spilled out the coffee he had been drinking. 'Art, you make the lousiest coffee I've ever tasted!'

'Ain't my fault, Rob,' Art Donovan complained. 'I figure that it's 'cause we let the horses piss in the creek afore I made the coffee that's wrong.'

* * *

Night closed in over Dane's Bend, bringing with it a tension that could almost be clutched out of the air. The carousing in the saloon had reached a pitch, and was at its most dangerous phase; the time when the hilarity waned and what had been joshing a short time before became the stuff of insult. Marshal Andy Daly had tried again to change Andrew Sloan's mind and tactics, but the banker had remained stubbornly steadfast in his conviction that the only way to protect the treasure entrusted to the bank was to recruit mercenaries, because he had no doubt that the Donovan brothers would come calling when Yancey Donovan failed to return to the fold. The one thing that could be taken as certain with the Donovans, was that they stood united.

'Too late to make plans when they're riding along Main, Marshal,' had been Sloan's final say on the matter.

Now, with an eerie stillness over the town, Andy Daly paced between his desk and the window. Some stragglers, obviously those not up to Sloan's standards, were being kicked out of the saloon by Ace Danagher, and therein might lay the spark that would ignite the fuse of trouble. One man objected to Danagher's forceful ejection and swung at him. Danagher, with a swiftness that hinted at many such encounters before, dodged the swinging fist and landed a jaw-breaker on the man that sent him spinning off the porch of the saloon and into the middle of the street. A second man, who seemed of a mind to weigh in in support of his partner, on witnessing Ace Danagher's swiftly delivered retribution, immediately raised his hands and backed off. However, Danagher did not let the man go scot free. As he turned to go down the porch steps, Andrew Sloan's chief enforcer put his boot on the man's backside and pushed. The momentum of the action pitched the already liquored man headlong into the street where he collided head first with the other man who was getting to his feet. Both men went down heavily, and stayed down.

As Danagher came down the porch steps, laughing meanly, and possibly of a mind to act in a more deadly fashion,

Andy Daly hurried outside and shouted, 'You've made your point, Danagher. Now back off.'

Ace Danagher stood stock still, his hand hovering over his sixgun. A million thoughts ran through Andy Daly's mind, but one was uppermost: could he outdraw Danagher if it came to it?

6

The marshal watched for the slightest change in Ace Danagher's demeanor, his mouth suddenly dry. Clearly, the hardcase was at a crossroads. The decision to draw or to not draw was taken from him by Andrew Sloan, who had come from the saloon.

'Ease back, Ace,' the banker ordered. 'We've got no quarrel with the law.'

Obviously not liking being reined in, Danagher bristled, but obeyed. He turned and went back into the saloon, angrily brushing past Sloan.

'You've got a tiger by the tail in Danagher, Sloan,' Daly said. 'Be real careful that he doesn't turn and devour you.' He turned his attention to the two men Danagher had kicked out of the saloon, struggling dizzily to their feet. 'You fellas OK?'

The older of the pair mumbled, and

Daly took that as an admission of a recovery of sorts. Supporting each other, the men wandered off in a zig-zag that took them from one side of the street to the other and back again.

Andrew Sloan had some advice to offer.

'Don't be a fool, Marshal. Danagher would have killed you, and I think you know as much.'

'No one knows for sure, Sloan,' the marshal said. 'Danagher's an unknown quantity round here.'

'Danagher's a killer through and through. His time in Dane's Bend is probably down to his need to keep a low profile while some trouble or other blows over. I hope that from now on you'll be sensible, Marshal. I might not always be on hand to rein him in.'

'How can you consort with a man like Danagher, Sloan?'

'You know, Marshal,' Sloan said, 'a banker and a hardcase such as Ace Danagher aren't all that unalike — in that we both profit from other people's misery.'

‘Peas in a pod, huh?’ Daly snorted.

Andrew Sloan laughed. ‘Well, I’d say more like snakes in a hole, Marshal.’ He settled his gaze on the marshal. ‘Talked to Henry?’

‘Yes.’

‘Good. Then you’ll know how little he can do. Join me for a drink, Marshal?’

‘I’d rather be struck down right this minute, Sloan,’ the Dane’s Bend lawman flung back, grim-faced.

‘Please yourself.’

The banker turned and went back into the saloon, his smug saunter leaving the marshal fit to be tied.

* * *

Rob Donovan stirred restlessly, unable to find sleep, growing more certain with each second of the long night that Yancey Donovan had run into trouble. Years of dodging had given him a keen instinct, and that instinct was now ringing alarm bells loud and clear. And, as the night passed, he swore to himself that had the town of Dane's Bend harmed his kid brother, it would pay a devil's ransom.

★ ★ ★

Sam Limbo was also tossing restlessly, having come from a nightmare in which an evil-faced monster was putting a noose around his neck, grinning at him with rotten teeth. It had surprised him that he had drifted into sleep in the first place, his mind being chockful with thoughts of Sarah Daly and what might befall her when the Donovans came looking for Yancey, which they would undoubtedly do. The lamplight from the marshal's desk glowed in his office, inviting ghosts to visit — particularly the Grim Reaper.

★ ★ ★

The light was a metal grey when the Donovans mounted up and made tracks for Dane's Bend.

7

'Ya know,' Spence Donovan groused, rubbing sleepy eyes. 'I'm goin' to skin that kid brother of mine alive if I find him in a dove's bed.'

'Stop your moanin',' Rob Donovan yelled. 'You should never have let him ride into Dane's Bend alone to begin with.'

'I couldn't do nothin' to stop him, Rob,' Spence complained. 'Yancey's ten times more stubborn than you when he takes it in his head to do somethin'.'

'That's the way it was, sure enough, Rob,' Art Donovan said. 'Me and Spence tried to stop him but he got in a real surly mood.'

'Yeah,' Spence said. 'Me an Art thought he was goin' to draw on us. Now, you wouldn't want that, would you, Rob?'

Rob Donovan was unimpressed by

his brothers' arguments. 'Two of you, one of Yancey. Seems to me you could have done somethin'.'

Spence Donovan, already in a foul mood, reacted angrily.

'If you wasn't off with that widder woman in Adam's Creek, pleasurin' yourself, maybe you could have lassoed Yancey. So don't blame me and Art.'

'You know, Spence,' Rob Donovan growled, 'Your mouth gets bigger every time you open it.'

Spence Donovan drew rein. 'You fixin' to close it, Rob?'

As many times before, Art Donovan stepped in to act as a peacemaker between his brothers, whom he was sure one day would not heed him and only one would walk away from such a bust-up. Normally they were united. But there were times, like in every outfit, when tempers got frayed.

'All that matters now, fellas,' Art counselled, 'is that we find Yancey. Any business 'tween you two can wait 'til that's done with.'

His long fingering worked once again.

'Art is right, Spence,' Rob Donovan said. 'Yancey first. Then you and me can face up to each other, if that's the way it'll pan out.'

Art Donovan reckoned that he had once more put off the evil day of his brothers' showdown. And, with any luck, as before, by the time they'd found Yancey, Spence and Rob would have gotten over their temper and they would ride out of Dane's Bend as brothers should, at one with each other.

* * *

As Sarah Daly made her way to the jail, bearing breakfast on a tray for her father and Sam Limbo, Ace Danagher stepped out from a crowd of sniggering layabouts the worse for wear after a night of slugging rotgut. Sarah had observed them from far off, and it had been obvious that Danagher's cohorts in Andrew Sloan's so-called bank security, were goading him in to making the move he now made to block Sarah's progress. She had thought about crossing the street to get past the gathering, but had decided that she was not going to be fazed by a bunch of troublemakers led by the town's biggest troublemaker of all — Ace Danagher.

A time or two since he had arrived in town, Danagher had tried to impose himself on her, but she had rebuffed his advances. Sarah had thought about telling her father about Danagher's antics but had thought better of it. Since his first day in Dane's Bend, when the marshal had suggested that the town had nothing to offer him and that he should hit the trail, Ace Danagher had been angling for a chance to tangle with her father and, were she to tell him about Danagher's ungentlemanly conduct which might after all be designed to engineer a confrontation with the marshal, it could be the catalyst to bring to the boil the bad feeling between the two men.

‘Why, Miss Daly,’ Danagher crooned, ‘I feel I have to do the gentleman and carry that heavy tray for you, ma’am.’

The men he had detached himself from watched with intense interest, because Danagher had boasted that Sarah Daly would not be able to resist his charm.

‘I don’t need your help, Danagher,’ Sarah said, caustically. ‘In fact I think you should crawl under the boardwalk to find company of your own kind.’

To a man, his cronies sniggered.

‘She sure is meltin’, like you said she would, Ace.’

Danagher pivoted about and landed a fist in the gut of the man who had spoken. The man doubled over holding his belly and spewed whiskey-stinking bile on to the boardwalk. The other men’s laughter ceased immediately and, to a man, they distanced themselves from the livid Danagher, forming a new huddle further along the boardwalk.

‘Get out of my way, Danagher!’ Sarah demanded.

'And if I don't?' he growled. 'What're ya fixin' on doin' about it?' He sneered. 'Maybe that old crock of a marshal will come to help his little gal.'

'You draw my pa into a fight, like you've been tryin to do since you showed your coyote ugly face in town, and harm a hair of his head and I'll kill you myself, Danagher. So help me God.'

He taunted her. 'Is that so? And how d'ya plan to do just that, ma'am?'

'Any way I can,' Sarah declared, with a steely resolve.

Ace Danagher began to crowd Sarah into the recessed door of the general store. 'I think I should get a little kiss for offerin' to help, Sarah. You reckon?'

Unexpectedly, and surprisingly, one of the men stepped forward.

'Leave her be, Danagher,' he said. 'You've had your fun.' Sarah recognized the dishevelled man as Larry Stritch who had been her father's first and, in the marshal's opinion, his finest deputy before rotgut robbed him of his decency. He tipped his hat. 'Sure sorry about this, Miss Daly.'

'Mind your own damn business, Stritch!' Ace Danagher barked.

'Ace is right, Larry,' said another man, fearfully. 'Ain't none of our business what Ace gets up to.'

'I guess your friend is right, Larry,' Sarah said, her heart full of pity for Stritch, and fear, too, for his safety if he pushed Danagher any further. 'But I thank you kindly.'

'You see, Stritch,' Danagher chuckled 'I think the lady likes the idea of givin' me that little kiss I asked for.'

Ace Danagher leaned towards Sarah and she recoiled, her face full of revulsion. She kicked him hard on the skin.

'I'd rather eat cow dung than kiss you, Danagher.'

Ace Danagher's mood notched up at least ten points in ugliness.

'You shouldn't have done that,' he said, rubbing his leg. 'Now I'm goin' to have that kiss, whether you like it or not.'

'I said let her be, Danagher.' Stritch stepped forward. 'Miss Daly is a respectable woman. Not the kind of saloon harlot you normally shack up with.'

Danagher swung around.

'I warned you to back off, Stritch,' he growled. 'And, dumb bastard that you are, you didn't. Now I still intend takin' that kiss, and if you want to stop me, well . . . ' Ace Danagher's hand hovered over his sixgun.

Stritch swallowed hard.

'Larry didn't mean nothin', Ace,' said the man who had earlier urged Stritch not to interfere. 'His brain's scrambled from liquor.'

'Stay out of it, Bennett,' Ace Danagher rebuked the man. 'Unless you want to stand 'longside of your pal.'

His courage fading, Bennett melted into the background under Danagher's glowering stare.

'You followin'?' Danagher questioned Stritch.

'I can handle this no-good just fine,

Larry,' Sarah said.

'I dare say you can, Miss Daly,' said the former deputy marshal of Dane's Bend, 'but you know, I've taken just about as much as I can take from you, Danagher.' His liquor-washed gaze hardened. 'As much as I'm going to take.'

Ace Danagher sneered. 'Say hello to the Devil for me, Stritch.'

'Touch that iron on your hip, and you can say hello to the Devil yourself, Danagher.'

Danagher swung round to find Andy Daly coming from the alley alongside the general store toting a cocked shotgun.

'I can handle him, Andy,' Stritch said.

'I guess maybe you can at that, Larry,' the marshal said, to give comfort to Stritch rather than having any belief in Stritch's ability to outdraw Danagher. There was a time in the past when Danagher would have posed no problem for his former deputy, but that time was long gone. 'But I don't want any show killings in my town. It's a long standing policy that you know well, Larry.

'Now, one of you fellas turn and walk away. And I figure that that man should be you, Danagher.'

'This is a big mistake, Marshal,' Danagher said, mean-eyed, as he strode away under threat of the lawman's blaster.

'Now, you in the opposite direction, Larry,' the marshal ordered.

Larry Stritch paused as he passed by Daly.

'I was about to get some of my pride back, Andy,' he said, and added bitterly, 'Damn you!' He marched off across the street angrily and straight into the saloon.

'You know, Sarah. Maybe I should have let Danagher put Larry out of his misery,' Andy Daly said. 'You OK?'

'Fine, Pa.'

'I saw Danagher's antics from the office window and came through the backlots, because' — his face saddened — 'there was no way I could face Danagher down, Sarah.'

Sarah put the tray on the boardwalk and hugged her father. 'Being fast with a gun is no mark of a man, Pa.'

* * *

Sam Limbo stopped his edgy pacing of his cell when Sarah and her father returned safely, relieved that Sarah was OK and, strangely, equally relieved that Daly was, too. Having suffered at the hands of lawmen who were no better than the men they were supposed to bring to book, and in many cases a whole lot worse, the honesty of the marshal of Dane's Bend rekindled his hope that one day soon the law across the West would be even-handed and honest in its dealings, and be enforced by men of Andy Daly's calibre. Strange, thinking about a man who would probably get him hanged, Limbo thought. But Daly was doing his job as he saw fit. Without that missing derringer and dishonest witnesses, there was nothing else the marshal could have done but arrest him for murder. 'Is that ham and eggs I smell?' he called out cheerily to Sarah, a cheeriness that was not returned.

'Is that all you can worry about, yourself, Sam Limbo?' Sarah flung back peevishly.

'That's all any man should worry about,' he retorted, unwisely.

'Is that so?' Sarah said. 'Well, when Judge Harding hangs you the world will be a better place, I reckon.' She slammed the tray down on the marshal's desk. 'You feed him if you want to, Pa,' she declared. 'But I reckon he might not be so selfishly inclined if his belly scraped against his backbone with hunger.'

Sarah spun on her heel and, on her fiery departure, slammed the door fit to bring the marshal's office down.

'You know, Marshal,' Limbo intoned, 'I've got a feeling that your daughter's sweet on me.'

Andy Daly frowned.

'That, Limbo,' he said, 'is what worries me more than anything else. But I figure that in a couple of days Judge Harding will relieve me of that worry.'

'Hang me and you'll be hanging an innocent man, Marshal.'

The marshal looked at Sam Limbo long and hard, his thoughts deep ones. He did not let Limbo know the outcome of his deliberations.

'I guess I'd better feed you,' he said.

'Much appreciated, Marshal.'

Daly took one of the plates from the tray and, taking the keys from his desk drawer, came back to the cells. 'Step right back to the wall, Limbo.' He had the key in the lock when a gun blast rocked the street outside. He dropped the tray and raced outside. He was back inside within minutes. 'Some damn fool fell over himself and his gun went off.' He felt a thud on the crown of his head. A weakness ran to his knees and he crashed to the floor, his eyes rolling.

'Sorry, Marshal,' Sam Limbo apologized. 'But leaving the key in the lock of my cell door was a God sent opportunity that I couldn't resist.'

Through a grey haze, Andy Daly watched his prisoner grab his gunbelt from the rack behind his desk and leave by the back door. He tried to get to his feet to follow, but the grey haze became a black shroud that enveloped him.

Sam Limbo edged up to the corner of the alley at the side of the marshal's office. Across the street there were three horses hitched to the saloon rail. As casually as he could, he sauntered across the street, pulling his hat low over his eyes to cover as much of his face as was possible. He unhitched one of the horses and was in the saddle when a voice called out from inside the saloon, 'Hey! That's my nag, mister!'

Sam Limbo spurred the horse and took off at a gallop, hot lead buzzing in the air around him.

8

Low in the saddle, Limbo flashed past the Daly house at the end of the main drag just as Sarah, alerted by the gunfire, came running from the house obviously worried that the lead-slinging could be directed at her father. But her concern swiftly changed to anger on seeing Sam, and then as swiftly back to worry, because if Limbo was riding helter-skelter out of town he could only be doing so by having broken out of jail. And her father would not have willingly co-operated in such a venture.

'Pa,' she screamed, racing along the boardwalk to the jail.

Sam Limbo wished he had time to tell Sarah that her pa had only suffered a bump on the head, but the lead buzzing around him left no time for anything but to quit Dane's Bend as fast as he could before the bullets chasing him from the men crowding out of the saloon ended his break for freedom. When he'd had time to think, he'd give some thought to the fact that now, along with being wanted for murder, he would also be hunted down as a jail-breaker and a horse-thief. And if he did not make it out of Dane's Bend now, he would most certainly hang long before Judge Harding arrived to give his hanging the stamp of judicial approval.

Glancing back over his shoulder, he saw the marshal come groggily from the law office, shooting. By the look of him, he could not hit the side of a barn. But that did not stop him chancing his luck. The men who had piled out of the saloon were mounting up. Most had to make several attempts to get in the saddle because the grog in their bellies was sinking fast to their legs. A couple simply fell out of the saddle as soon as they sat in it. But he could see at least a half-dozen men who were swinging their horses to give chase berated by

Ace Danagher for their actions, because the men riding out were part of the security outfit Andrew Sloan had hired to protect the bank.

As he cleared town, it concerned Sam when Andy Daly wobbled all over the place and fell straight into Sarah's arms. He truly hoped that the marshal's woolliness was not a symptom of a thin skull. He had not hit him that hard, merely to stun him. However, some men's heads cracked easier than others.

Looking more behind him than in front of him, when he turned in the saddle having strayed from the trail, a stout oak stood right in his path forcing him to draw rein and swerve in the one move. The awkward turn took it out of the mare and she lost some of her momentum for a brief spell, allowing the men in pursuit to close the gap. The mare picked up the pace again, but a whole lot of her friskiness had gone, and Sam Limbo wondered if she now had the stamina to remain ahead of the makeshift posse.

He checked again.

His pursuers had edged closer.

* * *

Sarah Daly helped her father into the marshal's office.

'Someone get Doc Lavery,' she called out.

Ace Danagher, by now having given up on any response from the men giving chase to Daly's prisoner, quickly saw a chance to ingratiate himself with Sarah, a woman who had been a source of temptation to him ever since he had set eyes on her the very first day he had ridden into Dane's Bend. His longing for Sarah was not motivated by the high ideals of love — no, Danagher's longing for the marshal's daughter was driven by lust.

'I'll rustle up Lavery, Miss Daly,' he called back, hurrying away to the town medico's house at the opposite end of the street to the Daly home.

'Thank you, Mr Danagher,' Sarah

was genuinely grateful, thinking that after all she might have painted Ace Danagher blacker than he was.

And that was exactly the sentiment Ace Danagher had hoped to spark in Sarah by his false act of kindness.

'My pleasure surely, Miss Daly,' he said. 'You just look after your pa.'

'What the devil are you playing at, Sarah?' her father berated his daughter. 'The last man I'd want help from is Ace Danagher.'

'You shush,' she scolded him, helping him to one of the cells where he could rest to await the arrival of Julius Lavery MD. 'And how the hell did Limbo break out anyway?'

Andy Daly confided his stupidity to his daughter, with a stern warning, 'I know, you know: no one else must know, Sarah.'

'I don't plan to go on any rooftop to announce that my pa has a hole in his head. Now lie down and be quiet.'

The marshal grinned.

'Just like your ma,' he said. 'Bossy to

the last, rest her soul.'

Sarah sat on the edge of the bunk. 'You miss Ma something terrible, don't you, Pa?'

Andy Daly sighed heavily.

'When your ma died there was a hole opened up inside me, Sarah; a hole that won't close until I see your ma again.'

Doc Lavery came rushing into the marshal's office, coming up short when he saw that Daly was alert. 'What's all the hullabaloo about?' the medic growled, in a voice that was like a rusty nail on tin. His eyes were more bloodshot than usual, hinting at the doc having fallen off the wagon he got on to at regular intervals. 'Ace Danagher almost busted down my door just now. Must admit that Danagher showing concern about you, Marshal, kind of rocked me out of the doze I'd slipped into.'

Doze? Daly thought. More like a coma, if the gunfire that chased Sam Limbo out of town had not woken him.

'I'm fine, just fine, Doc,' the marshal

said, standing up to prove it. He blinked, rubbed his eyes and blinked again. 'Except that there's four of you, Julius.' He laughed. 'Each critter uglier than the other.'

'Lie down,' Lavery ordered. 'I ain't in a humour for joshing.'

'You never are, you ornery critter,' Daly said.

Julius Lavery turned to Sarah. 'You must be a real saint to put up with a pa like you've got, young lady.'

'Sometimes it can be an ordeal, sure enough, Doc.'

Lavery returned his attention to Daly.

'Lie flat on your back, Marshal,' he ordered. 'I want to look in your eyes.'

Daly chuckled. 'Why, Doc, I never knew you cared.'

Sarah could not contain her laughter.

'I swear one of you Dalys is worse than the other,' Lavery growled, before a smile played on his lips. 'Any pain in that iron head of yours?' he enquired of the marshal, once he had examined his eyes and had them follow his finger.

'Just an ache.'

'Got a sizeable bump that'll be more sizeable still in a couple of hours.' Julius Lavery's fingers probed Daly's skull for any soft patch that would indicate a fracture, and concluded, 'Like I said, pure iron.'

Lavery looked around at the empty cells.

'That prisoner of yours seems to have stepped out,' he said.

Andy Daly grimaced. 'He'll be back in a little while, Doc. I'll be mounted up and riding shortly.'

'Not with that brain-shaking lump he gave you,' Lavery said. 'You need to rest for a spell, Andy. A longish spell at that,' he stressed.

'Fiddly, Doc,' Daly said. 'I've had worse in my time.'

'Doc Lavery is right, Pa,' Sarah scolded. 'You'd probably fall out of your saddle.'

'At least there's one Daly talking sense,' Julius Lavery said. 'And I pity her, having to deal with a mule-head like you,' he told the marshal.

Lavery fixed his gaze on Andy Daly.

'Are you still planning on squaring up to the Donovans?'

'And who says the Donovans are coming to town?' Daly growled.

'Just about everyone,' Lavery said. 'And I reckon that just about everyone is right, Marshal. You don't kill one of the Donovans and they do nothing about it.'

'Maybe the Donovans don't know that Yancey came to Dane's Bend, Julius,' Daly said.

'That's dumb thinking, Andy. Of course they know. They sent him ahead to scout. Probably have the bank in mind.'

'A nickel and dime bank like the one in Dane's Bend, wouldn't interest an outfit like the Donovan brothers, Julius.'

'Maybe they heard about whatever it is that Andrew Sloan has hired a private army to protect, Andy. Seeing that

Sloan, one of the meanest bastards this side of the Mexican border is parting with good dollars, it must be sizeable treasure.'

'In that case, the Donovans would have ridden in anyway,' Daly said disconsolately.

'Probably. But now, along with heisting the bank, they'll be looking to revenge Yancey.'

Marshal Andy Daly groaned. 'Revenging Yancey's death will be the sum total of their visit because by the time the Donovan brothers get here, I reckon Sloan's so-called security will have heisted the bank themselves.'

Julius Lavery snorted.

'I reckon so, too, Andy. And you'll be the biggest chump ever to come down the line if you try and stop them.'

'You're wasting your breath, Doctor Lavery,' Sarah said. 'Trying to talk sense into my pa is trying the impossible.'

'Well,' Lavery said, picking up his doc's bag. 'Just keep in mind, Marshal, that even a clever fella like me can't plug a hole in your head to stop your brains coming out.' He grunted. 'Even the small hole that that would take.'

His laughter drifted back from the boardwalk.

'Lavery's right, Pa,' Sarah pleaded. 'Why don't I ride over to Adam's Creek and ask the marshal there to come and help? He's got a deputy, too.'

'No, Sarah!'

'It would be the sensible thing to do, Pa.'

'Dane's Bend is my town. It's down to me to keep law and order here. How could I hold my head up if I go running to Jack Torrance over in Adam's Creek for help?'

Sarah, tears welling up in her green eyes, said quietly, 'A dead man doesn't need to hold his head up, Pa.'

9

'Come on, gal,' Sam Limbo coaxed the mare. 'We need to reach the cover of those hills.' He turned in the saddle to check on his backtrail and saw that if the mare kept slowing, his situation would soon be critical. It looked like some of the men who had formed the Dane's Bend posse had dropped out, but there were still four coming on with no sign of them giving up the chase. Luckily, the owner of the horse he had thieved had been careless enough to leave a Winchester in the saddle scabbard, but how many rounds were in it was as yet a mystery, and would remain so until he began shooting if it came to that. He turned and looked again to the hills which, to his alarm, if anything seemed to have moved further away.

The mare slowed more and more.

* * *

'I did the best I could, Mr Sloan,' Ace Danagher apologized to a very angry banker. 'Them dumb-heads just hared off, nothin' I could do to stop them.'

'You could have shot one or two, to knock sense into the others. I didn't feed those men free whiskey and pay them good dollars to do the marshal's work for him,' Sloan raged.

'It's kinda natural to give chase to a lowdown horsethief like Limbo,' Danagher said defensively.

Andrew Sloan stormed around his desk to come toe to toe with Danagher. 'What happens if the Donovan brothers ride into town while the men you were supposed to be ramrodding are off on a wild goose chase?' he snarled.

Ace Danagher moved back a couple of paces. Andrew Sloan might have the veneer of respectability, but underneath that veneer Danagher saw another man; the kind of man who would kill you as fast as he looked at you.

'We've still got plenty of men, sir,' he said.

'Danagher,' the banker said in a quiet voice, but one that was all the more unnerving for that, 'if I lose one dime from my bank because of your lackadaisical ways, I'll kill you.'

Ace Dangher had ridden trails with rough-house hardcases who'd put a scare into Satan himself, but in all his time he had not come across a man as terrifying as Andrew Sloan. He reckoned that that was because a man expected a black heart in a hardcase. However, to find the blackest heart of all dressed up in the expensive duds of a banker, sent a shiver as cold as a dead-man's touch along his spine.

'Get out of my sight!' Sloan roared.

Ace Danagher came from Sloan's house at the same time that Sarah Daly left the marshal's office. Mean of mood after being dressed down by the banker, he reckoned that it was time he collected his dues for his good deed in getting Doc Lavery to attend to her pa.

And this time, he'd not take no for an answer.

* * *

Miraculously, the mare was still going. When it looked like she was all tuckered out a couple of times, Sam Limbo's sweet talk had given the horse new life. The foothills of the wooded slopes were now within reach, and once he got up into the timber, Limbo reckoned that his chances of survival would be greatly enhanced.

He looked back. The four riders of the hastily formed posse were still coming on hard and fast, no doubt anxious to catch up with him before he reached the cover of the trees. If he reached the timber the chase would turn to a game of cat and mouse, the outcome of which would probably be decided by luck.

'Ain't far to go now,' Sam Limbo softly cajoled the mare. 'Just one more spurt of energy should do it, gal.'

* * *

Preoccupied with thoughts of her father's dilemma, Sarah Daly did not see Ace Danagher until he sprang from a shadow.

'Howdy, Sarah,' he crooned. 'You sure look pretty.'

Sarah had just left the end of the main street and there was not a soul around to help her and, seeing the gleam of lust in Danagher's eyes, help she would need, she reckoned, because the fire glowing in Ace Danagher's eyes was that of a man beyond the limits of his control.

'What do you want, Danagher?' she questioned him, striking a brave pose which she was far from feeling.

'What do I want?' he sniggered. 'A little appreciation for gettin' Doc Lavery to your pa so quickly, Sarah. Now don't that deserve a little reward?'

'When the bank opens tomorrow, you'll get your reward, Danagher.'

Ace Danagher's scowl darkened and

his eyes, if possible, glowed even more hotly with the fire of lust.

'How much do you reckon your help is worth?'

'I ain't talkin' about no money!' he growled. 'Why, I had me a little womanly comfortin' in mind, Sarah.'

'I told you before, I'd rather kiss cow dung, Danagher,' Sarah spat. 'And nothing's changed since.'

She went to go past, but Danagher stepped in front of her. 'Is that so, Miss high-and-mighty Daly? Well' — he came towards Sarah — 'I reckon that if you ain't givin', then I gotta do the takin'.'

* * *

Sam Limbo breathed a sigh of relief as he climbed into the trees, tall stout pines that would stop a cannonball let alone a bullet. The topography of the hills, with its many trails within trails, would be to his advantage. He had covered a lot of territory in his travels, and had learned to use terrain to his advantage. And he was hoping that the men pursuing him were, in the main, town-dwellers who would not be able to match him in reading the lie of the land. He was hoping that with luck favouring him he could avoid the men altogether and give them the run around until they tired and gave up. He would prefer not to get involved in a shooting war, because he saw no point in killing needlessly. However, if the oncoming riders started the shooting, he would be left with no alternative but to defend himself.

So far they looked a determined bunch, but Limbo was hoping that their grit was whiskey-driven and, as they sobered, they would lose the anger that had stoked their pursuit.

Sam Limbo climbed a trail through the trees to a point from where he could monitor the posse's progress, and was relieved to see only three riders now, one less than the previous count.

* * *

Ace Danagher grabbed hold of Sarah Daly and dragged her into a nearby shed. Her struggle was cattish and Danagher's face suffered her clawing. She kicked out at his shins and bit his ear, but the fight in her only excited Danagher all the more.

'You're a real she-cat, ain't ya?' he chuckled. 'But I like a woman with fire in her.'

He tried to kiss her, but Sarah spat in his face. He slapped her hard and sent her reeling backwards. He was on her like a wild animal. Stunned from the blow, the fight had gone out of her.

'Ain't had me a woman in a long time,' Danagher said. 'And I ain't never had a woman like you, Sarah.'

'My pa will kill you, Danagher,' Sarah said weakly. Her head was clearing and her fight was coming back, but if she were to escape Ace Danagher's foul attention her next attack on him had to come as a complete surprise.

'Your pa will kill me?' he sneered. 'I don't think so. 'Cause the second I see him, I'll sink lead in his gut.'

Sobbing, Sarah lay back feigning acceptance of her lot. The next time she struck out would be her last chance to escape Ace Danagher's evil clutches. And if she did not make it count, then she would prefer to die trying.

'Who knows, Sarah,' Danagher sneered, 'ya might like it!'

10

Nearing the foothills, another man in the dwindling posse sobered enough to realize the dangers of riding blind into the trees. As he slowed, the two other men in the trio slowed also.

'What's the matter, Charlie?' one of the men asked, but already knew the answer to his question.

The rider whose good sense was overcoming his liquor-induced bravado drew rein. 'That jail-breaker really ain't none of our business, fellas. His snarin' is a job for the law.'

'He's a damn horsethief,' the man who had questioned Charlie bellowed. 'And horsethieves need hangin'.'

'Dan is right,' said the second man of the trio, still flushed with whiskey.

'You go ridin' into them hills, and you might not be comin' back out,' Charlie argued. 'This fella Limbo is gun-slick. I seen him draw on Archer, and he's fast. Should never have been in jail an'way.'

'What're you talkin' about, Charlie Bellows?' asked the man called Dan.

'I seen that derringer ev'ryone says Archer hadn't got,' Bellows said. 'Seen it with my own two eyes, fellas.'

'Makes no diff'rence,' Dan growled. 'He's a horsethief.'

'Never would have been no horsethief if he got a fair break,' Bellows countered.

'So if you saw this derringer, why'd ya keep your mouth shut, Charlie?'

'No one else said nothin'. Why should I stand out? I gotta live in Dane's Bend.'

'So how come no derringer was found, huh?'

'It wasn't found 'cause in all the excitement, Lubelle hid it up her pettitocats,' said Charlie Bellows.

'Makes sense, Ned,' Dan said to the third man in the trio. 'Archer was a regular visitor to Lubelle. And she had a real soft spot for Archer, too.'

'How do you know that, Dan?' Ned questioned.

'Well . . . ' Dan shifted uneasily in his saddle.

'Annie told him,' Charlie said.

'Shut your mouth, Charlie,' Dan growled, 'or I'll shut it for ya!' He addressed Ned. 'I'm not a fella given to visitin' saloon doves, Ned. But since my wife busted her hip, she ain't been in the humour.'

'Your problems are yours, Dan,' Ned said curtly. 'Is what Charlie says true?'

'Yeah. Annie told me that Lubelle had dreams 'bout Archer and her shackin' up together,' Dan confirmed.

'The town lawyer shackin' up with a saloon dove,' Ned laughed. 'More likely that the moon would fall to earth, I say.'

'That's why I reckon Lubelle hid the derringer away. She wanted this fella Limbo to hang for Archer's murder, 'cause in her mind Limbo had killed her man,' Charlie Bellows speculated.

'Women!' Ned snorted. 'Can't trust

'em. But' — he settled a steely eye on Charlie — 'we still got ourselves a horsethief to hang.' Bellows swallowed hard. Ned Scott could be a real ornery critter sober, but liquored up his temper knew no bounds. 'You lost your tongue, Charlie?' he snarled.

* * *

From his vantage point, Sam Limbo observed the dispute between the men hunting him, and it gave him hope that if the argument was divisive enough, they would turn tail and head back to Dane's Bend. One of the men had turned and was riding away, obviously having changed his mind. That left only two, a very agreeable reduction of the odds, Limbo thought. On seeing the departing man tumble from his saddle, clutching at his back, Sam Limbo reckoned that all hope of avoiding spitting lead was gone, because the men now coming forward again were obviously of a killing mentality.

* * *

'No need for roughness now, Ace,' Sarah said, opening her arms to Danagher, whose surprise at the turn of events had his jaw dropping. Sarah's look was a smouldering one. 'You're right, Ace, maybe I will like it at that.'

'Sure you will, honey,' Danagher crooned, breathless with the pleasure to come.

She pulled him down on her before he could unbuckle his gunbelt, in a show of pagan passion that stole every scintilla of caution from Danagher. As her arms entwined him, Sarah grabbed his sixgun and poked it into his side. Having been made to look a sucker, Ace Danagher's anger knew no limits.

'I'm goin' to tear you limb from limb, Sarah Daly,' he vowed.

'If you move, other than to get your filthy person off me,' Sarah said with a steely resolve, 'I'll put a hole the size of your dumb head in your side,' she promised.

Ace Danagher's rage almost made him fatally foolish.

Sarah prodded the barrel of the sixgun deeper into his side.

'I'll do it, Danagher,' she stated. 'Of that you can be certain. Now, ease yourself off, stand up, turn and leave.'

Danagher did as she said, but added a snarling promise of his own, 'This ain't over.'

Sarah got to her feet, making sure that the Colt .45 never wavered, and her eye didn't shift a smidgen away from Ace Danagher.

'I reckon your best move now would be to hit the saddle and clear out while you still can. Attempted rape in a western town will earn you a quick noose.'

By his reaction to Sarah Daly's statement, it was obvious that Ace Danagher had already thought about the outcome of his encounter with the marshal's daughter, once she broke news of it. Reaction to such a heinous offence would be a hot-blooded one, and he could be dragged off to the nearest tree, pronto.

Thinking as he was, he knew that Sarah Daly had to be silenced. And though in his conniving lifetime there had not been many moments of honesty with himself, Danagher now knew that her murder, once he'd taken his pleasure, had always been at the back of his mind to save his neck from being stretched.

That Ace Danagher had not immediately complied with her order, unnerved Sarah because she was not at all sure that if he chose to continue with his aggression that she could pull the trigger of the sixgun. It took a special kind of courage to kill someone, and she was not convinced that she had it. 'If you're still here in the blink of an eye, you're a gonner,' she said, with a bravado she was far from feeling.

Ace Danagher, having lived through

many threats, had become expert in spotting the slightest hesitancy in an opponent, even hesitancy masked by bravado. And though Sarah Daly was quite the actress, he could sense the slippage in her resolve to do as she had promised she would.

'Ya know,' he said, taking a couple of steps towards Sarah, 'I figure I might hang 'round for a spell longer, Miss Daly.'

Sarah aimed the sixgun firmly at Danagher's belly. 'Do, and you'll hang around permanently, Danagher.' But her words, even to her own ears, held more hope that Danagher would relent, rather than the resolve to act if he did not.

'Now, honey,' her tormentor drawled lazily, 'you know that you're not goin' to use that gun. So why don't you give it to me 'fore you hurt yourself.'

'I'll use it, Danagher,' Sarah said, but her threat sounded empty and hollow, and only served to put Danagher on a firmer footing than he had already been.

'Enough of this nonsense,' he growled, and strode towards her.

Sarah Daly's finger shivered on the trigger of the Colt .45.

'Damn you to hell, Ace Danagher,' she said.

Danagher's eyes popped. Had he underestimated Sarah Daly's grit to do exactly what she had threatened she would?

11

As the remaining two riders who formed the makeshift posse came on, Sam Limbo's hope of avoiding gunplay went up in smoke. Not a killer by nature, Limbo was troubled by the thought. He reasoned that if they got the chance they would try to kill him, and he would have to defend himself. However, the logic of his reasoning did nothing to ease his conscience. The truth of the matter was that had the patrons of the saloon in Dane's Bend acted as witnesses to Benjamin Archer's treachery, by now he'd be riding another trail without a care in the world instead of getting ready to engage in a shoot-out.

Sam Limbo's mind slipped back to the cross-roads a couple of miles outside Dane's Bend that had four signs, any one of which, other than the sign for Dane's Bend, had he chosen that way, would have set him on another course. But Limbo consoled himself with the thought that life was a deck of cards from which each day a new hand was dealt — some hands you won, and some hands you lost. And he hoped that he was not holding a losing hand now.

The riders far below his vantage point, rode into the foothills and were momentarily lost from view. But Sam Limbo was not worried. To find him they would have to come into view a hundred times again to challenge him. And every one of those hundred times, he would have them in his sights.

* * *

Marshal Andy Daly came to the door of the marshal's office to watch Sarah as she made her way along a street that was getting steadily more rowdy, and it surprised him that she was not in sight. It had only been a couple of minutes since she had left, and she would have to have moved with the speed of a mountain cat to have reached home. She had a couple of friends living along the main street on whom she might have called, he supposed, but the thought only gave him a brief respite from his concern; a concern which reached a new keenness on seeing men spill out of the saloon, legless and itching for trouble of one kind or another. There was the crash of breaking furniture inside the saloon, raised voices and angry exchanges. As he had anticipated, the free liqour that Andrew Sloan had used to recruit his mob was taking a predictable course. The dispute inside the saloon reached new heights with the shattering of the window by a chair that struck one of the men who had come from the saloon, on the shoulder, making him storm back into the saloon shouting, 'Who flung that damn chair!' Ready to become embroiled in the ruckus.

The Dane's Bend marshal was

caught between concern for his daughter and intervention in the saloon bust up which, by the heated exchanges, was on the verge of becoming a pitched battle. Further along the street, nearer the bank, Andrew Sloan came to his front door to gaze worriedly towards the saloon. Andy Daly had little sympathy for him. He had started out on a road against all advice; a road that could only lead to big trouble. And how big that trouble would become was now being hinted at.

The marshal's indecision was set aside by the thunderous crash of gunfire from the saloon.

* * *

The same echo of gunfire also made Ace Danagher pause mid-stride. And Sarah Daly, concerned for the safety of her father had her concentration on Danagher diverted who, quicker to recover from his surprise, took full advanatage of Sarah's dropping of her guard to wrench the sixgun from her grasp. She clawed at him, but Danagher possessing none of the finer qualities, struck out and landed a fist on the side of her head that spun her back against the wall of the shed with such force that her head snapped back to collide with the wall.

She gasped and slid to the floor.

Ace Danagher cursed his luck now that he had Sarah Daly at his mercy a second gunblast required his immediate investigation. Leaving Sarah unconscious, he fled the shed.

* * *

Sam Limbo had the lead rider of the two remaining from the Dane's Bend posse in his sights, when he heard voices coming from another trail to the left of where he lay in waiting. He could neither see the approaching riders nor hear what they were saying. Limbo slid down off the flat rock he was on and slipped back into the dense scrub behind him, from where he could still see the oncoming riders. Limbo figured that riders who chose the trails through the hills rather than coming across the less hazardous plain, would be men who wanted to make their journey to their destination as far as was possible, unseen.

Men like the Donovan brothers.

Sam Limbo checked on the two men from the posse and reckoned that any minute now they would come face to face with the other riders.

* * *

Ace Danagher had no sooner come from the shed where he had left Sarah unconscious, than he realized the foolishness of his move in leaving her alive to tell the tale. There was plenty of trouble in town and lots of fellas the worse for liquor to pin the murder on. He was about to return to the shed to finish her off when Andrew Sloan hailed him.

'Danagher,' the banker bellowed angrily, 'what the hell am I paying you for? Sort out the trouble in the saloon. Now!'

'Yes, Mr Sloan, sir,' he called back.

'You're being paid to see that this kind of thing doesn't happen,' Sloan rebuked his enforcer.

'I told you it would, Sloan,' Andy Daly shouted above the din. 'What you're witnessing now is the end result of free rotgut.'

Danagher hurried along the street to the saloon. By now the brawl was spilling out on to the street and men were throwing punches left right and centre at everyone around them, most of them too drunk to distinguish between friend and foe, and it was only a matter of time before some outraged drunk began shooting.

'Do something, Daly,' the banker demanded. 'You're the marshal.'

'I've been the marshal all along, Sloan,' Daly growled, 'but you figured I couldn't handle the trouble that might come along. Looks like you and your rowdies ain't doing so good right now.'

'I'll settle 'em down, Mr Sloan,' Danagher said.

'Do, or you're out of a job, Danagher,' Sloan promised.

Ace Danagher weighed into the fighting men throwing them aside and slinging haymakers at any man who was not prepared to listen to his exhortations to cease brawling. One man, toppled down the porch steps by Danagher's left fist to land on his backside in a mound of horse manure, sprang to his feet, his face a mask of scowling rage.

'You had no call to do that, Danagher,' he challenged the hardcase hotly.

Danagher, sensing deadly danger in the drunk's challenge, swung round, his gun already clearing leather. The man who had challenged Danagher had his gun unholstered but it didn't matter, Danagher's bullet ripped through his chest and out through his back. The dying man staggered back, spun round and fell. His finger jerked the trigger of his pistol in a reflex action and Andy Daly screamed out. His right leg buckled under him, the man's wild bullet having fractured it.

* * *

Sam Limbo watched with interest as the two groups of riders converged. There were three in the unseen group and Limbo recognized the oldest of the men as Rob Donovan — Yancey Donovan's older brother. Obviously, by the aggressive attitude of the two Dane's Bend riders, they were not aware of the deadly men they had confronted.

'Ain't room on this track to pass,' said the man called Ned Scott. 'Move aside into that clearing.'

Sam Limbo reckoned that he might have one less enemy to worry about in a second from now. Rob Donovan and his brothers had killed men for much less than Scott's brash demand. But it was Spence Donovan who responded.

'Don't think me and my brothers are of a mind to oblige, friend,' he said. 'But if you want to press your point . . . ' Spence Donovan rested his hand on the butt of his .45.

Ned Scott, still full of whiskey-induced bravado ignored his partner's attempt to silence him.

'I ain't takin' no lip, Dan,' Scott railed. 'Right is ours, I reckon.'

'Stubborn old windbag, ain't he, Brother?' said Art Donovan, addressing Spence.

'Stubborn old windbag, am I?' Ned Scott fumed.

Scott's partner grabbed his wrist as his hand dropped to his sixgun. 'Ned don't mean no offence, sir,' he said urgently. 'He's had a gutful of whiskey and he ain't right in the head, you understand, don't ya?' he asked hopefully.

'Let go of my damn gunhand, Dan,' Scott growled. 'I ain't 'fraid of these bozos!'

Ned Scott's partner was pale before, but now his weakness made it necessary for him to grab his saddlehorn to remain in the saddle. Clearly, he had recognized, or cottoned on to the identity of the men Scott was goading so brazenly.

'You don't want to start trouble with these gents, Ned,' Dan managed to croak. 'We'll just move aside, huh,' he said to Spence Donovan.

'You lily-livered bastard, Dan Croker!' Scott bellowed. 'I ain't budgin' one inch from this spot.'

Rob Donovan addressed Croker. 'Seems like your friend is hankerin' to catch lead, mister. Only so much a man can take' — his gaze settled on Spence Donovan — 'before he tires of tryin' to reason.'

'You're a reasonable fella,' Art Donovan told Dan Croker. 'No need to throw in your lot with your jasper of a partner.'

'There sure ain't, mister,' said Dan Croker, distancing himself from Scott.

'Ya know what, Croker,' Scott raged. 'When I'm finished with these fellas, you'll be next to catch my lead.'

'Ned,' Croker pleaded, 'these fine men are *brothers*.'

'I don't give a damn!' Scott snorted. He chuckled. 'Save on graves. They can all go in one.'

'I figure that somewhere along the line,' Spence Donovan said to Dan Croker, 'your saddle partner's brains fell through a hole in his head.'

'Ned!' Croker pleaded.

'I've had enough of your butt kissin', Croker,' Scott roared.

'*Brothers*, Ned,' Croker repeated.

Ned Scott looked at Dan Croker through eyes dulled by liquor, his befuddled brain trying to make sense of information that should have sent alarm bells ringing.

'*Brothers*; you understand, Ned?' Croker implored.

Ned Scott laughed. 'Like I said, I don't give a . . . ' Scott's whiskey-dimmed eyes suddenly came to vibrant life as his dulled brain finally made sense of Dan Croker's message. The blood drained from his face and he shook in the saddle.

The Donovans laughed.

'Heh, I'm sure sorry,' Scott apologized. 'Me and Dan will just let you gents pass, huh?'

'You took the brunt of this idiot's abuse, Spence,' Rob Donovan said, 'so I figure what happens next is your call, Brother.'

'That's mighty generous of ya, Rob,' Spence Donovan said, rubbing his stubbled chin while casting a mean eye over Ned Scott. 'What d'ya figure we should do, Art?'

'Kill them both, of course,' was his reply.

'Got any ideas on how we should do that?' Spence asked.

'Well, I'd be for skinnin' them both alive,' Art Donovan said. 'But time is short. So' — he drew his pistol — 'tell ya what, Spence, you shoot the yahoo who's been givin' ya grief. And I'll blow his partner's head off his shouders.'

Spence Donovan looked to the oldest Donovan and the boss of the outfit. 'How does that settle with you, Rob?'

Rob Donovan shrugged.

'Like I just said, Spence. It's your call.'

'Wait a minute.' Dan Croker distanced himself further from Ned Scott, leaving him stranded. 'I didn't insult no one. It's Ned was doin' all the mouthin' off.'

'The man's got a point, Spence,' Rob Donovan said.

'Sure I do,' Croker said, grasping at the smidgen of hope Rob Donovan had held out.

Spence Donovan made a pretence of considering his older brother's reasoning. Watching, Sam Limbo saw the cruelty of Spence Donovan's charade. He had no intention of letting either man off the hook Scott's mouth had hung them on. But, like a cat toying with a mouse, it gave the outlaw pleasure seeing the Dane's Bend man's hope taking root, only for it to be snatched away in the second before Spence Donovan killed him. And the scenario he was witness to gave Limbo one hell of a dilemma, because he reckoned that he could not stand idly by and let two men be murdered in cold blood. However, there was the fact that if the Dane's Bend men had successfully cornered him, they would have had no hesitation in killing him. Or hauling him back to Dane's Bend to swing at the end of a rope that he didn't deserve. So he owed them nothing. When the killing was over, the Donovan brothers would go on their way, and he could do the same and cross the border to lie low for a spell until it was safe to return stateside. However, he had no sooner decided on that course of action than his conscience pricked at him and Sam Limbo knew that whatever the outcome, he would have to step in.

He was about to break cover when

Ned Scott spoke up, and his words changed everything.

'We've got a trade to make,' Scott said, breathless with fear.

'A trade, huh?' Spence Donovan said. 'Now what would two saddlebums like you have to trade to gents like me and my brothers.'

'Ah, let's just plug 'em and ride, Spence,' Art Donovan groused. 'They ain't got nothin' worth tradin', for sure.'

'We're waitin',' Rob Donovan said a spell later, when Scott's fear had made his mouth too dry to speak.

Dan Croker supplied the answer Scott was incapable of making, 'Ned and me know who killed your brother Yancey.'

The Donovans sat rigid in their saddles.

'Did you say *killed*, mister?' Rob Donovan checked.

'Yeah,' Croker confirmed. 'That's what I said, sure enough, Mr Donovan. Shot Yancey down dead centre of main in Dane's Bend, just as Yancey was mindin' his own business ridin' outa town.'

'Has my brother's killer got a name?' Rob Donovan enquired of Scott.

'His handle is Limbo. Sam Limbo,' Croker lied.

12

Limbo might have stepped barefoot on a rattler when he heard the lie.

'Obliged, friend,' Rob Donovan said.

'Limbo, huh?' Spence Donovan said.

'You know him?' Dan Croker asked, his fear eased on hearing Rob Donovan's gratefulness.

'We know him,' Spence Donovan confirmed.

'Then you'll know him for the killer he is,' Ned Scott said.

'That's the strange thing, you see,' Spence Donovan said. 'Limbo is a rogue and a ruffian, but never reckoned on him being a cold-blooded killer. Ain't his way.'

Dan Croker and Ned Scott, sensing a shift of ground again, exchanged wary glances.

'Well, if he wasn't before, he darn well is now,' Scott said, shakily.

Spence Donovan looked long and hard at the Dane's Bend pair. 'Maybe you fellas killed Yancey and are spinnin' a yarn to save your hides.'

'We never!' Dan Croker yelped. 'Limbo rode into town and got into a game of blackjack. Shot a fella for cheatin' in cold blood. He was no cheat. Then when your brother was ridin' out he shot him.'

'And robbed him, too,' Scott lied. 'Took his winnin's right from out of Yancey's pocket, and him just dead.'

'If Limbo killed this gambler in cold blood, as you say,' Art Donovan pitched in, 'then how come the law hadn't locked him up before he got to kill Yancey when he was ridin' outa town?'

Croker and Scott exchanged alarmed glances, because they were tying themselves up in knots and hadn't the answers to undo those knots.

'That's a very good question,' Rob Donovan said. 'And I'm waitin' for a convincin' answer,' he added menacingly, his eyes hooded and mean.

'The Dane's Bend marshal ain't up to much,' Scott croaked. 'Ran scared of Limbo.'

'Me and Ned's got somethin' else to trade, too,' Croker said desperately, under close scrutiny from the Donovan trio.

'My ears are open,' Rob Donovan said.

'There's somethin' mighty big in the Dane's Bend bank safe.'

'That's old news,' Spence Donovan said. 'A Mex 'fraid of trouble south of the border stashed his pile in the Dane's Bend bank, we heard. That's why Yancey was in town, to try and confirm if what we heard down Sonora way was true. Ya see, Yancey had charm by the bucketful, and could get folk to talk when no one else could.'

'It's true, sure enough,' Croker said. 'Andrew Sloan, he's a banker in Dane's Bend, has hired a private army, expectin' you fellas to drop by. Figurin' that when you heard about Yancey, you'd wanna make the town pay.'

'This fella Sloan got that right,' Art Donovan said. 'Hope your town's got a big cemetery, 'cause by the time we settle with Dane's Bend it's goin' to be near to full.'

'We can help you fellas,' Ned Scott volunteered.

'Appreciate that,' Rob Donovan said. 'Why don't you men lead the way?'

'Yeah,' Scott said warily. 'But it would be a whole lot nicer if we all kinda rode side by side, don't you reckon, Mr Donovan? Now that we're pards.'

Rob Donovan chuckled. 'Are you fellas afraid we'll shoot you in the back?'

'Heck, no,' Dan Croker piped up.

'That's good to hear,' Spence Donovan said. 'So' — his sixgun flashed from leather — 'we'll shoot you as you sit.'

The Colt spat twice.

'Now that ain't fair, Spence,' Art Donovan complained. 'You was only supposed to shoot one of them critters, Brother.'

'Ain't it a fact, that sometimes I get carried away,' Spence laughed. 'Well, best make tracks for Dane's Bend, I guess.'

'No. We'll wait,' Rob Donovan said.

'Wait?' Spence questioned the gang-leader. 'What for? You was all fired up to get to Dane's Bend, Brother.'

'Yancey is dead. So we've got time. We'll ride in before first light when the town is in dreamland. Bust open the bank, and then burn the town down around them while they sleep.'

'Now that sounds like a real good plan to me, big brother,' Art Donovan sniggered.

* * *

Sam Limbo had had two strokes of luck. The first had been that in their fear, the Dane's Bend duo had not revealed why they were in the hills. And the second was that the Donovans had not thought it of any interest to them that they should ask.

The Donovans, not being aware of his presence, gave Limbo the chance to slip away, but it was a chance that could also backfire, because his horse was hitched at the end of a scrub-covered slope through which he would have to crawl to reach the mare. A long dry spell had made the scrub tinder dry, and its brittleness prone to rustle or snap with the slightest brush against it. Which meant that, though the slope was not a long one, it would be the longest he had ever traversed, because in the eerie quietness of the hills, the snap of a twig or a rustle of brush would alert the Donovans to him. Being outlaws, always on the alert, their ears would be trained to pick up the smallest sound. He could risk waiting until the Donovans bunked down, but that would be a risky strategy to adopt. The distance between him and the outlaws was not far, and all it would take was for one of the Donovan brothers to come his way to relieve himself to be discovered. And it would be a long, anxious wait. The other alternative would be to launch a surprise attack on the outlaws, but Sam Limbo reckoned that that would be no better than cold-blooded murder, which would not settle well with his conscience. And the longer he lived, the heavier the burden of guilt would become. Not a prospect he'd look forward to. So all that was left was to risk a belly crawl down the slope, and hope that fate would give him a third stroke of luck.

13

Back in Dane's Bend, Marshal Andy Daly was rolling in the dirt of the main street almost out of his mind with the pain of his bullet-fractured leg, after the wild shot from the man Ace Danagher had gunned down. Danagher's pleasure at Daly's misfortune was immense. He had been worried about the lawman's reaction, should Sarah Daly have made known his deeds. The marshal would have then been a man driven by rage, and that always, in Danagher's experience, made a man even moderately gun-handy difficult to overcome, because rage chased away fear and caution. He reckoned that he had the measure of Daly with gun skill to spare. However, with mob law firmly taking hold of the town, he did not want to have Daly to deal with as well as Andrew Sloan's hirelings. He had a plan that no one but he knew about, and that plan was to rob the bank himself that very night and be long gone before the Donovans arrived in town.

Facing up to the murderous Donovans had never been an option. With his scheme in mind, he suggested to Sloan, 'Maybe it would be wise to have a couple of fellas inside the bank tonight, Mr Sloan. Looks like this town is cuttin' up badly.'

Sloan was not about to let a couple of cut-throats into the bank on their own.

'That's a good idea, Ace,' he agreed. 'How about you and me?'

The banker's suggestion set Danagher back apace. He'd prefer the company of men of his own kind. A couple who were well liquored up and easy to cut their throats.

'I was reckoning on O'Leary and McGraw, Mr Sloan,' Danagher said. 'Never figured on you wanting to lose your sleep.'

'You know best, Danagher,' Sloan said, making a pretence of placing full trust in the hardcase. 'After all, you know your own kind.'

The banker's slur did not settle with Ace Danagher, and another time he'd have gunned him down there and then. However, the thought of getting his hands on whatever booty Sloan had been prepared to pay top dollar to protect, had the hardcase smiling broadly, as if Sloan had paid him the highest compliment.

'Wise thinkin', Mr Sloan, sir,' he said. 'O'Leary and McGraw are, as you say, my kind.'

'Better get the marshal to his house,' the banker said, 'before he wakes up the entire cemetery. I'll send Doc Lavery along, if he's not so far gone from liquor that he's more dead than alive.'

'Sure, Mr Sloan.'

Andrew Sloan studied his henchman, and pondered again the thoughts he'd been pondering for some hours now, and wondering how far he could trust Ace Danagher in a partnership he had almost proposed when Danagher had advised him that a couple of men should be put in the bank overnight. He was a wealthy man in his own right, but he had grown weary of Dane's Bend and the ignorant and culture-starved West in general, and his feet itched to live in the kind of more elegant societies found in Europe. And with that in mind, he reckoned that the Mexican's fortune entrusted to his care, added to his own, would make life in Europe mighty pleasing. His plan would be to make the robbery of the bank look like the work of a man like Ace Danagher. That would let him free of any hint of impropriety, because he would need to leave America with a blemish-free pedigree if he were to be accepted, as he longed to be, in European society.

But how much would Danagher want to be part of his plan? And, more important still, how far could he trust Danagher to stick to a bargain struck? Of course, there would be one other problem after the robbery and that would be Danagher, alive and able to talk in the future. Or maybe even blackmail him in the future. So of necessity for a peaceful mind, Danagher's post-robbery existence would have to be a short one.

'Somethin' botherin' you, Mr Sloan?'

The banker became aware of Danagher's close scrutiny. In his pondering, his study of Danagher had slipped, which had allowed the hardcase to study him in turn.

'Bothering me?'

'You were kinda off somewhere else, sir,' Danagher said.

Ace Danagher wished that he could read the banker's mind because, from a long history of connivance and underhandedness, he recognized in Sloan a man who had a head chock full of devious thoughts. And he was pretty sure that in those thoughts, he played a prominent part. But what part? That was the question.

'Haven't you arranged for the marshal to be carried to his house yet,' Sloan barked.

Danagher knocked a couple of heads together to form a bearer party to take the marshal to his house. He followed along, pretending to supervise the procession, but nearing where he had left Sarah Daly he drifted off into the shadows and waited until it had gone on a safe distance. Then he took a knife from his boot and slipped into the shed.

⋆ ⋆ ⋆

On hearing the jingle of spurs round a bend just ahead, Sam Limbo pulled back into the shadow of a ledge with only seconds to spare. Art Donovan came into sight, peering into the grey gloom. Limbo pressed back as far as he could against the rockface, and hoped that the shadow of the ledge would be deep enough to hide him. If not, the outlaw would have a clear and deadly advantage, because if Limbo fired his pistol, Art Donovan's brothers would be warned of his presence. And with them having that knowledge, his chance of getting out of the hills by stealth would be gone.

Why was Art Donovan wandering around in the first place? Limbo had thought that he had escaped the outlaws' attention, but had he? His passage through the scrub had been painstakingly slow and meticulously careful. But, of course, men like the Donovans had instincts as sharp as a needle point, and perhaps it was the alerting of those instincts that put Art Donovan on the prowl. The danger was, that if Art was on the prowl, then maybe his brothers were also. But soon, on hearing the slap of reins close by, it became clear to Sam that the dark figure crouched low in the saddle of the approaching horse, on the blind side of the ledge and therefore out of Art Donovan's sight as yet, was probably the reason for the outlaw's prowling about.

The clatter of a stone alerted Art Donovan to the rider's presence. The outlaw crouched low, gun drawn and lined up on the rider who, in a couple of seconds would come into Donovan's sights. If Sam did nothing to warn the man, he'd ride into certain death. And if he did act, he'd probably be added to the toll of dead in the hills, because unnerved, the rider, along with Art Donovan would open fire and he would be in the centre of deadly crossfire.

Sam had a sense of his luck deserting him.

* * *

Ready to do the deed of murder he had come to do, Ace Danagher went directly to where he expected to find Sarah Daly unconscious, only to find her gone. Panicked, his eyes searched every inch of the dark shed until they came to rest on a section of the rotten wall where a couple of planks of wood had been prised loose, creating a hole big enough for Sarah to have escaped through. But why had she not left by the door to the street? The answer was simple. On inspection he found that from the shed a path led directly to the back yard of the Daly house.

Sarah Daly had made it home, and that meant all sorts of trouble for him. The marshal, injured as he was, posed no threat to his wellbeing. But that would not be the case when Sarah made his treachery public knowledge.

Ace Danagher ran a finger inside the greasy collar of his shirt, already feeling the tightness of a lynch rope. Should he hit the trail? Or start the open revolt he was certain he could start; trouble that would bring chaos to the streets of Dane's Bend, and in the midst of that trouble take his chance to raid the bank and escape before anyone realized that he was missing?

* * *

Deciding that he could not possibly let the unknowing rider ride into an ambush, Sam Limbo saw no alternative but to warn him. He was about to holler when a rifle cracked from atop of the ledge he was under. The rider came out of his crouch and sat ramrod straight for a moment, before he toppled forward off his horse.

'Got him, Art,' Spence Donovan called out.

'Damn it, Spence!' Art Donovan groused. 'I wanted to see the surprise on his face when I shot him. Ain't ya goin' to leave your little brother any fun no more?'

'Stop your moanin' and get back to camp,' Spence said.

Sam Limbo stood stock still, not daring to draw breath until the sounds of the Donovans' retreat faded. Concerned for the rider, the instant it was safe to break cover he did so and went to the man's aid. It was a waste of time. Spence Donovan had put a bullet in the man's brain. A silver star was pinned to the man's chest. Peering closer, Sam Limbo recognized the sheriff of a town called Sinkwell, about thirty miles east of Dane's Bend. Limbo remembered Jack Lace as a fair lawman. Obviously he had been tracking the Donovans, but why Limbo did not know. And neither did it matter now.

14

Sarah Daly's first concern was the injury to her father and, with his welfare in mind, she had made her way by the path that led from the scene of her ordeal at the hands of Ace Danagher to the house to be waiting as if nothing had happened when he arrived. Suffering as he was, she did not want to burden her father with knowledge of what had happened. Ace Danagher she would take care of herself, as soon as her father was resting at ease.

Before she slipped into the house, made aware of her father's injury by overhearing remarks by the men carrying him, Sarah caught sight of Danagher at the spot where she had prised loose the rotten wall boards of the shed to make her escape, and it worried her that he could throw caution to the wind to try and silence her before she spoke out. He hadn't much to lose. He would know that in Western towns would-be rapists got swift justice.

He could not act while the men who had carried her father to the house were still around. Nor could he do so while the doctor was tending to the marshal, but after that the way would be clear for Ace Danagher to quieten her. Now she worried that she had also put her father in mortal danger. Danagher would not risk her secret being revealed, and that meant that her father would have to be silenced also, in case she had confided in him. And Andy Daly being helpless, it would not take much for Danagher to do that. But Danagher's problem would be in trying to guess how long it would be before the marshal's daughter thought it safe to speak out. He would probably count on having time, because Sarah would not want to add to her father's worries. But how long would he safely have would be Danagher's concern.

During that period he would grow ever more edgy, ever meaner and, with every passing second, ever more dangerous.

Sarah Daly's thoughts turned to Sam Limbo and how she wished that she could now go to the jail and release him. And it surprised Sarah that she had no doubt at all that Sam would have helped her. Though she had a mountain of trouble to deal with, it surprised her also that her thoughts of Sam Limbo should be as warm and as sweet. After all, he stood accused of murder, was a jailbreaker and horsethief.

Concentrating on her immediate tasks, Sarah hurried around lighting lamps before the marshal was delivered home, and generally creating the impression that she had been home since shortly after leaving the marshal's office twenty minutes before. Passing a hall mirror she gasped in horror on seeing the swell of her face where Ace Danagher had struck her. In no time at all the swelling would blacken, and then there would be no hiding what had happened to her. She hurried back the route she had come and quenched most of the lamps, in the hope that the shadowy house would help to hide her injury and stave off the inevitable questions that would follow, should her injury be noticed.

* * *

Limbo waited until he was certain that Art and Spence Donovan were clear of the area, before he began to make his way down the timbered slopes. Making his way out of the hills would bring with it many dangers, any one of which could immobilize him or see him drop into a gully or ravine. He would also have a horse to get safely through the many obstacles that might arise. The night would be moonless which was a drawback in unfamliar terrain. But the intense darkness would also protect him from prying eyes. Because, though his main worry was the Donovan brothers, the hills might also be home to others of a like nature. The Sinkwell lawman might have been tracking the Donovans, but on the other hand his quarry might have been some other desperado, and his meeting with the Donovans could just have been an unlucky twist of fate.

He needed to have a wide gap between him and the men on his tail by sun-up if his plan to make it back to Dane's Bend ahead of them was to work out. Dane's Bend? Where had his plan to make tracks for the border changed to one of returning to a town that wanted to hang him unjustly? The reason for his return to Dane's Bend did not take much figuring out. There was only one reason.

Sarah Daly.

The thought of a beautiful woman like Sarah falling into Donovan hands churned Sam Limbo's stomach.

15

Andrew Sloan had finally arrived at a plan, and with that plan in mind he was visting Henry Wilkins.

'It's late, Andrew,' Wilkins was saying. 'I was on my way to bed.'

'What I ask won't take long, Henry,' Sloan pressed.

Wilkins shook his head. 'What you think is crazy, Andrew.'

'Probably is. But I'll sleep a whole lot better if you tell me that, Henry.'

'Counterfeit bonds, you say?'

'They look counterfeit to me, Henry.'

'But Manuel Sanchez is one of Mexico's finest citizens, Andrew.'

'I'm not saying that Sanchez is peddling bogus bonds, Henry. I reckon that they were off-loaded on him, and he didn't recognize them for what they are — useless paper. Very fancy useless paper, but useless nonetheless.'

'But how did you come across these bonds, Andrew?'

'I was checking to see if everything was OK for the night ahead, when the fakeness of these bonds caught my eye. Of course, you're a bond expert, Henry, and I might be talking out of my rear end. That's why I'd like you to come along and look them over.'

'I must, of course,' Henry Wilkins said.

'While you're getting dressed, I'll go on ahead.'

When Andrew Sloan left the Wilkins house, he walked in a straight line until he was sure that if Wilkins was watching, he'd be satisfied that he was going to the bank by the normal route and not through the backlots to the rear of the bank. With this in mind, as soon as he thought it was safe, Sloan ducked into an alley and quickly made his way to the bank and let himself through the rear door to wait for Henry Wilkins's arrival, when he would implement the first part of the plan he had hatched to leave Dane's Bend with Manuel Sanchez's fortune.

He sat in the dark, not wanting to draw attention to the bank by lighting a lamp, which would be the excuse for the darkness he would give Henry when he arrived. Wilkins would be the easy part of the plan. Danagher would be more tricky, because where Henry Wilkins was the trusting kind, Ace was of the suspicious variety and would more quickly, given the merest hint of treachery, cut his throat.

* * *

Sam Limbo was relieved to see the trail widen out as he reached the end of the hills. The mare had not been in the best of shape to start out with, and now she was even more wobbly-legged. Having to nurse, coax and cajole the mare, it would be a long and slow ride to Dane's Bend. There would be long stretches where he'd have to walk to unburden the mare; time he would use to hatch a plan, not having as yet the slightest idea as to how he was to survive the Donovans and the law.

Limbo would have preferred to have waited until near first light to start out on the return journey, but had he done so, the fine stallions the Donovans rode would get them to Dane's Bend long before him.

* * *

Ace Danagher was getting more anxious by the second, and most of that anxiety sprang from the fact that he could not make up his mind what to do. His every instinct told him to mount up and ride hell-for-leather, but there was robbing the bank to consider. He had decided that for one reason or another, probably not to worry her pa distressed as he already was, Sarah Daly had kept her mouth shut. If she had spoken up, he'd probably be swinging in the breeze by now. How long would her silence hold? Enough time to rob the bank?

Reaching a decision, he left the shed from where he had been watching the

Daly house, and made his way to the bank.

* * *

'Andrew,' Henry Wilkins called into the darkness of the bank when he entered, 'are you here?'

'Sure I am, Henry.'

Startled, Wilkins swung around to find his banking partner behind him.

'Why no light, Andrew?'

'Didn't want to attract attention, Henry.'

'But I can't examine the bonds without light,' Wilkins complained.

'Oh, I think we can forget about examining the bonds, Henry,' Sloan said quietly.

'Forget? I don't understand, Andrew.'

'Never figured you would, Henry,' Sloan said.

Henry Wilkins's eyes popped, and his breath left him in a whoosh as the knife Andrew Sloan was holding pierced his heart. He tried to clutch at Sloan, but

Sloan stepped back and let Wilkins crash to the ground. Then Sloan dragged the dead man to his office and sat him in his chair, alongside the safe that would, come morning, be found open, unlocked and empty with Henry Wilkins's own key. To that end, Andrew Sloan took the key from his pocket and put it in the lock of the safe where it would be found. He also dipped his fingers in Wilkins's blood and placed the blood on the key. Then he left the bank to enact the second phase of his plan to enrich himself.

He let himself out the same way he had entered. He was on his way back to the alley to reach the main street when he saw Ace Danagher coming stealthily towards him. He ducked into the shadows to wait and see what the hardcase was up to. It did not surprise Sloan any when Danagher made a beeline for the rear of the bank.

'If you're planning on breaking in, I can help you, Danagher.'

Ace Danagher's gun left his holster

like greased lightning on hearing Sloan's voice.

'Easy,' the banker said, showing himself.

'I was just checkin' that ev'rythin' was all right, Mr Sloan,' Danagher lied.

Andrew Sloan laughed smugly.

'Do you expect me to believe that, Danagher?' he crowed. 'You were planning on breaking in to try and get your hands on the riches in the bank safe. And' — Sloan crossed the backlot to come face to face with his hireling — 'like I said. I can help you to do just that.'

'I'm not sure I'm hearin' what I think I'm hearin',' Danagher said.

'Sure you are. But in case there's the slightest doubt, I'm saying, let's rob the bank together, Danagher.'

* * *

Sam Limbo's thoughts were coming together, and he had a plan.

16

Ace Danagher's jaw was on his chest.

'You want to rob your own bank, Sloan?' he checked.

'That's what I'm proposing,' the banker confirmed.

'Now, why would you want to do that?'

'Simple. To get my hands on more money than I could earn in a lifetime of banking. Or' — he sighed — 'ten lifetimes of banking in this backwater.'

'Somethin', I don't get, Sloan . . . '

There would be a lot that Ace Danagher wouldn't get if it needed a brain to figure it out, Andrew Sloan thought. But his friendly smile showed no hint of his disparaging thoughts.

'All you've got to do is walk in there,' Danagher continued, pointing to the bank behind him, 'open the safe, take the money and vanish. So why d'ya need me to help ya?'

Sloan's last thought about Danagher's intelligence was off the mark, unless he had had a one-off brainstorm.

The banker put an arm round his hireling's shoulders, and explained. 'Because, my friend, when I leave Dane's Bend I want to wander free and unencumbered. And the only way I can do that is if the law is looking for someone else.'

'Me, huh?'

'You,' Sloan confirmed.

'And why would I want the law looking for me and not my partner?' Danagher questioned.

'How much have you got in your pocket right now, Danagher?' Sloan asked.

'A coupla dollars.'

'Now if you could turn that couple of dollars into' — the banker thought for a moment — 'oh, say ten thousand dollars?'

'T . . . ten . . . ' Ace Danagher stammered.

'Ten thousand dollars,' Andrew Sloan repeated. 'That, my friend, will be your fee for being the sole thief. I'll be the victim, and leave Dane's Bend half crazed after my bank's been robbed.'

Andrew Sloan saw the glint of greed he expected to see in Danagher's mean eyes.

'Ten thousand, huh,' he piped up. 'I figure that that ain't enough to have a posse of lawmen, bounty hunters too, I reckon, on my tail.'

Andrew Sloan went through the pretence of being outraged.

'I figure that, oh, twenty thousand might be just about right,' Danagher proposed.

'Fifteen,' Sloan bargained.

'Eighteen,' Danagher countered.

'Seventeen. Not a penny more, Danagher,' the banker stated.

'Seventeen and a half.'

Andrew Sloan played the game. 'That's extortion!'

Ace Danagher sniggered. 'That's business, Sloan.'

Sloan took a moment before agreeing, 'Seventeen and a half, it is.'

Ace Danagher was a mighty pleased man. He'd be leaving Dane's Bend with a whole lot more than he had expected when he had ridden in a couple of months previously. And the icing on the cake was that his booty was risk-free.

'So what now?' he enquired of Sloan.

'Now we rob the bank; I pay you off. Then you'll leave town on a fast horse, to make folk wonder why that is. I'll immediately check on the bank and find that it's been robbed, and dance a jig like you've never seen it danced before, my friend. Everyone will recall your leaving on that fast horse and . . .

'Well, you get the picture, don't you?'

Danagher chuckled. 'Ya know somethin', Sloan, you're more crooked than I am.'

Andrew Sloan laughed and slapped Danagher on the back. 'Why should that surprise you? I'm a banker, Ace.'

Laughing, Sloan led Ace Danagher into the bank.

‘Seventeen and a half thousand dollars,’ Danagher sighed.

‘Seventeen and a half thousand dollars,’ Andrew Sloan confirmed.

Not a cent of which Ace Dangher would collect. That was phase three of Andrew Sloan’s plan.

* * *

Sarah Daly looked in on her father who was sleeping restlessly and groaning a lot. Closing the bedroom door gently, she went back downstairs and into the parlour where Doc Julius Lavery was nursing a bottle of rye.

‘A fine whiskey, Sarah,’ he said, raising his glass in salute when she entered the room. It worried her that Lavery should be getting drunk when her father might need him, but there weren’t many days now, since Mary Lavery had passed on, that Julius wasn’t liquored up to some degree, and a lot of days when he was out cold. ‘Your pa’s leg set well,’ he said, understanding Sarah's unease. 'He'll have a bit of a limp, I reckon. But not much. I've seen men lose a leg altogether with less of an injury, Sarah.'

Lavery looked more closely at her.

'That bruise on your face will be ugly,' he said. 'Danagher?' And, when Sarah reacted, 'Who else? Dangaher's been lusting after you since he first set eyes on you, Sarah.' He gave a short little cough. 'Nothing *happened*, did it?'

Sarah shook her head.

'Good.' Julius Lavery set aside his glass. 'Mind if I curl up on your sofa?'

Pleased that he had stopped drinking, and that he'd be on hand should her father need him, Sarah Daly readily agreed to his request.

'Thanks for everything, Doc,' she said.

Stretched out on the sofa and on the verge of sleep, Lavery said, 'Pity that fella Limbo isn't here, isn't it, Sarah?'

He started to snore.

'Yes,' Sarah said quietly. 'It surely is a pity, Doc.'

* * *

'I'll get the spare key to the safe,' Andrew Sloan said to Ace Danagher. 'It's in Henry Wilkins's office.'

'The key to the safe is just lyin' around?' Danagher questioned, mystified.

'Not just lying around,' Sloan said. 'Hidden.'

'Ain't you got a key to the safe?'

Andrew Sloan, crossing to Wilkins's office, paused mid-stride. 'Sure I have. But the safe has a double lock. It needs two keys to open it: mine and Henry's.'

'Two locks,' Danagher grunted. 'Clever that. Don't think I ever seen a safe with two locks.'

Andrew Sloan said with a wry grin, 'It makes the bank harder to rob.'

Ace chuckled. 'Unless a gent can get his hands on both keys, that is.'

Sloan continued on, careful when he opened the door to the office to make the angle acute enough to rule out any chance of Danagher seeing the murdered Henry Wilkins. Once safely inside, Sloan rubbed his right hand in Wilkins's blood and hurried back outside. He held up his key to the safe, the only one needed to open it, crossed to Danagher and grabbed him by the arm, pressing his bloodstained hand firmly against his jacket to form a good impression.

'Let's rob the bank, Ace,' he said cheerily.

A moment later, Ace Danagher had a puzzled look when he saw Henry Wilkins sitting in his chair. He swung around to face Sloan who rammed a sixgun into his chest and fired in the same instant, giving Danagher no chance to cry out because his heart was shattered. Having the barrel of the gun right against Danagher's body had also muffled the sound of gunfire. In the rowdy atmosphere of the town, he could probably have fired a cannon, but Andrew Sloan was not a man to take chances. He crossed to the window looking out on the main street to check if there was any sign of attention being focused on the bank and, seeing none, he returned to the safe and cleaned it out into a cloth sack which he had left ready. He then left the bank by the rear door. He discarded the cloth sack in a load of debris a little further along the backlot, from where he would collect it when the town quietened down. It made him uneasy to leave his new found riches behind him, but it was a risk be had to take to give legitimacy to the robbery. He then made his way along the alley that led to main, paused at the corner to check the street, and then at an opportune moment crossed the street and regained his composure before strolling along to the saloon where he joined in the brouhaha going on for a couple of minutes, before asking if anyone had seen Ace Danagher. The reply to his question was inconclusive, which he had expected it to be from a crowd of drunks. He then made his excuses to leave, making a point of saying that if anyone saw Danagher to tell him to come along to the bank where he'd be waiting, and where Danagher was to join him to watch through the night.

Letting himself into the bank, he counted to ten before he ran outside shouting, 'The bank's been robbed and Henry Wilkins has been murdered!'

Within moments a crowd flooded into the bank.

'Someone light the lamps,' a shocked Andrew Sloan shouted over the excited din.

When the lamps were lit, the true horror of what had happened was revealed in all its gory detail. And the centrepiece was the open, cleaned-out safe. Sloan quickly explained how he had thought that some of the bonds in the bank's treasure trove were fake.

'I asked Henry to check them out, to verify what I suspected,' Sloan explained. 'He must have been here when Danagher broke in and forced him to open the safe. There's blood on the safe key. Henry's, I reckon.'

He side-stepped to get closer to Ace

Danagher, raising the lamp he held to shed light on him. Then: 'Look.' He bent down to examine the bloodstain on Danagher's arm. 'Henry must have struggled,' he intoned in horror. 'And Danagher gutted him. But Henry must have managed to get to the sixgun he kept in his desk drawer to shoot Danagher.'

Heads were nodding in agreement.

'But . . . ' Andrew Sloan's brow furrowed. 'Danagher could not have acted alone. The bank has still been robbed. Danagher had accomplices. Anyone see riders leaving town?' The banker's eyes scanned the shaking heads.

'We'll form a posse at first light, Mr Sloan,' a man called out.

'Thank you, Mr Flaherty,' Sloan said.

Rounding up a body of men, many of whom were drunk or as good as, Flaherty said, 'Let's get the marshal to deputize us right now, gents.' And turning back to Sloan: 'We'll get the bank's money back, Mr Sloan.'

'Do, and I'll make it worth every man's while,' Andrew Sloan promised.

* * *

Sarah Daly was woken from a doze she had slipped into by hammering on her front door. When she opened it, men flooded in, led by Jack Flaherty who informed Sarah, 'The bank's been robbed, ma'am. We're forming a posse and we need the marshal to deputize us.'

'You can't see my father now,' Sarah protested.

'We've got to,' Flaherty insisted.

Julius Lavery came blur-eyed from the parlour. 'Sarah's right. The marshal's in no fit state to have visitors.'

'Then who'll make the posse legal?' Flaherty asked.

'Legality didn't trouble anyone when a posse hunted down Sam Limbo,' Sarah pointed out, heatedly.

'Don't upset yourself so, Sarah,' Lavery advised. 'In the absence of the marshal, I reckon the town doctor will do to swear you men in as deputies.'

'That's good enough for me,' Flaherty said. 'Start deputizing, Doc.'

* * *

The first grey light of dawn was creeping over Dane's Bend when Sam Limbo arrived on its outskirts to the sound of hoofs clipping it. He pulled into a stand of trees on the edge of the town to watch the posse ride past helter-skelter, and he was powerless to stop them. Being a wanted man they would likely shoot him on sight or string him up. The Donovans would be riding into Dane's Bend, and every able-bodied man was riding out.

Limbo dismounted and put his plan into action. It was a simple plan, but one that he reckoned would work better than any complicated scheme. He had to enter the town incognito. He rolled in the dust to make his clothes look tramp-like. Then he used the same dust to camouflage his face. He ripped the sleeve of his shirt and the brim of his hat. Tussled his hair so that it poked out from under his hat, and finally and, painfully, put dust in his eyes to give them the bloodshot appearance of a drunk. Now all he needed was an empty whiskey bottle, and the new character he had created would come fully to life.

Stumbling along the main street there was no shortage of empty whiskey bottles, and picking one up he went and sat near the saloon. Head bowed, he started to mumble the way a drunk would. The only people around were stragglers from the night's revelry in the saloon.

An hour passed before the Donovan brothers showed up.

There was no sign of the marshal, and the law office was locked up. He wondered why that was, seeing that the Donovans had been expected.

17

The Donovans rode along the main street of Dane's Bend unconcerned, confident that there was nothing to worry about. However, seeing Sarah Daly come to the door of her house as they passed by gave Sam Limbo a whole lot to worry about. Further along the street a furtive Andrew Sloan caught his eye, ducking back into the livery on spotting the Donovan brothers. A natural thing for any man with sense to do, when the Donovans were coming. But there was something about Sloan that was different, but what it was Sam Limbo was at a loss to understand.

Skulking was a word that came to mind to describe the banker's manner.

'Cute,' Art Donovan said, riding past the drunk on the saloon porch, referring to Sarah Daly.

'I get first go, little brother,' Spence

Donovan said. 'Redheads are my bailiwick.'

'Keep your mind on the job,' Rob Donovan growled.

The job, Limbo quickly discovered, when the Donovans drew rein outside the bank, was to rob the bank. When the Donovans went inside, Andrew Sloan was quick to mount up and ride out. He was half way along the main drag when the Donovans charged angrily out of the bank on to the street. Sloan had to veer away, and not being an expert horseman the mare stumbled, throwing him. A cloth sack tied to the banker's saddle horn ripped, spilling the proceeds of the bank robbery on to the dusty street. Bereft, Sloan tried to grab as much of the treasure that he could.

'Looks like we found us a bank robber,' Rob Donovan said, and shot Sloan in the head.

Money retrieved and saddle-bags stuffed, Spence Donovan said, 'Now, I think while you fellas are burnin' this burg to the ground, I'll pay me a visit to that filly we saw as we rode in.'

'That's not a very good idea, or a very smart one either.'

The Donovans swung ground to find Sam Limbo behind them.

'And who might you be to tell us what's smart or not?' Art Donovan screamed. 'You filthy drunk!'

'I'm your fellas' ticket to hell, friend,' Limbo said, sixgun flashing from leather to blast Art Donovan first and Spence Donovan second.

Rob Donovan's hand froze on his sixgun.

'That's evened up the odds,' Limbo said and, holstering his gun, added, 'Anytime you feel lucky, Donovan.'

Rob Donovan drew and almost got Sam Limbo, his bullet nicking his left shoulder. Another couple of inches in, and it would have punched him in the heart. Rob Donovan was not as lucky. The top of his head vanished. Blood spouted into the air. The last of the Donovan brothers fell on his back, dead.